SPIRIT'S KEY

EDITH COHN

SQUARE
FISH

FARRAR STRAUS GIROUX
New York

SQUARE
FISH

An Imprint of Macmillan
175 Fifth Avenue
New York, NY 10010
mackids.com

SPIRIT'S KEY. Copyright © 2014 by Edith Cohn.
All rights reserved. Printed in the United States of America by
R. R. Donnelley & Sons Company, Harrisonburg, Virginia.

Square Fish and the Square Fish logo are trademarks of Macmillan and
are used by Farrar Straus Giroux under license from Macmillan.

Our books may be purchased in bulk for promotional, educational, or business
use. Please contact your local bookseller or the Macmillan Corporate and
Premium Sales Department at (800) 221-7945 ext. 5442 or by e-mail at
MacmillanSpecialMarkets@macmillan.com.

Library of Congress Cataloging-in-Publication Data
Cohn, Edith.
    Spirit's key / Edith Cohn.
        pages cm
    Summary: Having finally developed the psychic ability her father has used
to provide for them, twelve-year-old Spirit Holden, aided by the ghost of her
beloved dog Sky, investigates the mystery of why wild dogs are dying on their
remote island.
    ISBN 978-1-250-07969-5 (paperback)   ISBN 978-0-374-30012-8 (ebook)
    [1. Psychic ability—Fiction.   2. Dogs—Fiction.   3. Animal ghosts—
Fiction.   4. Single-parent families—Fiction.   5. Fathers and daughters—
Fiction.   6. Islands—Fiction.   7. Mystery and detective stories.]   I. Title.

PZ7.C66493Spi 2014
[Fic]—dc23
                                                                                2014012867

Originally published in the United States by Farrar Straus Giroux
First Square Fish Edition: 2016
Book designed by Andrew Arnold
Square Fish logo designed by Filomena Tuosto

1   3   5   7   9   10   8   6   4   2

AR: 3.9 / LEXILE: 590L

For Jer and our fur daughter Leia

TABLE OF CONTENTS

MR. SELNICK'S FUTURE

WHEN I GET HOME FROM SCHOOL, EVERY cabinet in the kitchen has been thrown open. There's a mess in the living room, too.

"Looking for something?" I ask Dad.

He runs his hands through his normally neat hair, which at the moment sticks frantic in every direction. "Have you seen the candles?"

"I think they're in my room. I'll check. Is the power going to go out?"

Dad shakes his head. "Someone's coming for a reading."

My heart flip-flops with excitement. "Eder Mint?" Eder used to be Dad's best client. But not even Eder has been in for a reading lately. It's been two months, the longest stretch without business since we moved to this island. That was six years ago, before people came to trust that what Dad sees, happens.

"No, Mr. Selnick. He's coming any minute," Dad says, "and I need those candles."

I dash to my room. Most everything we own is hidden in boxes. Dad likes to order supplies in large quantities. His stockpiling has created mountains of cardboard that rise up every wall.

Each room in our house is painted a different color, and mine is purple. These days, though, I have to lean my head *waaay* back to see the color, because Dad's mountains go *waaay* up.

I dig fast, cutting the packing tape off box after box. "Found them!" I yell. Dad doesn't mess around. There are enough candles here to light

the whole island. I grab two, along with a bur-
gundy bedsheet.

"What's that?" Dad eyes the bedsheet with sus-
picion.

"I thought it might look nice draped on the
table." I shake out the sheet and cover the dinky
card table with it. "See?" I stand back to admire it.
"Now you have a little atmosphere."

Dad frowns and mutters something about
mumbo jumbo. Candles, atmosphere, and crystal
balls are what Dad calls mumbo jumbo. That
stuff is for hacks, and Dad is not a hack. He asks
to hold a person's house key, the kind you use to
open your front door, and as soon as the key is in
his hand, *bam!* He *knows*.

It used to be that simple.

It used to be Dad didn't need mumbo jumbo.

"You're tapping into your power, is all," I insist.
"And it might help to dress things up a bit." I place
the candles inside two holders and arrange them
in the center of the table. "Nice, right?"

"I'm tired just looking at it," Dad says.

I snap my fingers. "Coffee. You need coffee." I rush to the kitchen to make him a pot.

Dad also didn't use to need coffee in the afternoon. But lately nothing's like usual. Dad is tired. He has trouble concentrating, and usually this soon after school I wouldn't be home to help him. I'd be out with my dog, Sky, running up and down the sand dunes. Or swimming in the ocean. Or bicycling, with Sky running alongside, or . . .

Well, the point is I'd be with Sky. And Dad would be breezing through his readings instead of scrunching up his face, worrying he won't get it right.

When the coffee is finished, I bring Dad a cup, but he doesn't drink it. He catches a glimpse of himself in the hall mirror. He tucks in his shirt and presses down his hair. He restacks some boxes to make them tall and orderly.

Finally, he sits down and takes a deep breath, but his foot doesn't stop tapping. There's sweat inside the wrinkles on his forehead, and when

Mr. Selnick bangs on the door, Dad knocks over a chair standing up to answer.

When Mr. Selnick comes inside, I set the chair back upright. The big man takes off his hat and plops down like he's relieved to have the weight of the world off his feet. "Thanks, honey," he says.

My name isn't Honey. It's Spirit. Spirit Holden. But Mr. Selnick calls everyone honey. Mr. Selnick is our neighbor three houses down and one across. I wonder what's up. Dad has regulars, and then there are people who come only if something's wrong.

Mr. Selnick hands Dad his house key, which is my cue to skedaddle. But my foot lands on one of Sky's squeak toys. It makes the worst kind of noise in the silence and brings back the pain of Sky's death like a crashing wave.

Dad doesn't notice. He's busy lighting the candles. The light reflects off the bedsheet and casts a strange red color on Mr. Selnick's face.

I pick up the squeak toy, a stuffed pheasant. Sky's things are still the way they were when he was alive. The pheasant seems to look at me sternly with its yellow-stitched eyes, like it would disapprove if I threw it away. It was Sky's favorite toy.

I set it on the bookcase. I'm about to leave, but I pause when I hear Dad say something about a baldie.

"I don't think this dead baldie in your yard means a negative future for you personally." Dad scratches his head. "But I'm not sure."

I shouldn't eavesdrop. Dad caught me once when I was little, and he said listening to his private readings was like peeking at someone's diary. *Holding a person's key,* he said, *I see everything they lock up. People trust me with their most private secrets.*

Even though I wouldn't tell anyone, it isn't fair for me to know Mr. Selnick's inner secrets.

But another dead baldie? Baldies are what people call the wild island dogs. We have bald eagles, too, which is how Bald Island got its name. But people call eagles sacred creatures. The dogs are the baldies, because they're unique to our island. No one else in the world has dogs like ours.

Sky was a baldie. And anything to do with Sky has to do with me, so I don't leave. I press up against the wall next to the bookcase with Sky's pheasant.

"Not sure?" Mr. Selnick asks. "Is there something wrong with my key? This one's a copy. Victor made it for me. Did Hatterask mess up my key?"

"No, no, your key's fine. Don't worry." But Dad pushes Mr. Selnick's folded money back across the table. "This reading is on the house."

Dad never does readings on the house. His readings *pay* for our house and every box in it. I get that same sweaty feeling I got the day Sky wasn't waiting for me after school. Like something's bad wrong and I need to stick my head in the freezer to cool off and think clear.

Mr. Selnick is about twice as big as Dad. His gut sticks out under his folded arms like a shelf, and his large shoulders square back like he means not to leave until Dad spits out something more specific. "Whatever it is, you best lay it to me straight."

Dad takes a sip of coffee, then picks up Mr. Selnick's key again. He closes his eyes and begins to rock. Back and forth. Back and forth. Then he shakes like he's cold, shivering until he jumps up and drops the key on the table like it burned him. "There's danger ahead."

"Dag-nab-it! I knew that baldie paws up in my yard was an omen." Mr. Selnick shakes his finger at the air. "I told my wife: *The devil's after us.*"

"Get Jolie and the kids. Pack your bags."

"What?" Mr. Selnick looks dumbfounded.

Dad walks to the door. "You have to leave the island." He stares hard at Mr. Selnick. "Tonight."

2

MY TODAY

"LEAVE THE ISLAND?" MR. SELNICK REPEATS, AS if Dad can't possibly be serious. He lifts his large body out of his chair like he's got time to spare. "I've lived on this island since I set foot on this earth. I'm not a-goin' anywhere. If the devil wants me, he knows which house is mine."

But after a moment, Mr. Selnick doesn't look so sure. He picks up his hat and twists it like it's wet and needs wringing. "What did you see? Tell me what I'm up against so I can be ready."

"The best advice I can give you is your own," Dad says. "Leave this island."

I suck in a breath and hope this means what I think it means.

"I told you I'm not a-goin' anywhere." Mr. Selnick shakes his head. "I never said I was."

"I saw your face covered in dirt so black I almost didn't know it was you," Dad says. "You were wearing the same blue plaid shirt you're wearing right now, and you turned to Jolie and said, *We should've left the island.*"

I'm so relieved I almost let out a whooping wowzer right there and turn myself in for eavesdropping. A real vision! This is the kind of reading islanders have come to expect from Dad.

"I intend to die here just as I was born." Mr. Selnick puts on his hat like it's some kind of statement to permanence.

Dad nods. "I understand. Our keys are an important reminder of who we are and where we live. But I'm required to tell you the truth as the key told it to me."

That's the problem with the gift. People don't always get the future they want. One time when Dad gave someone bad news, he and I had to leave town. That's how we came to live on Bald Island. This little boy got hit by a car. Dad saw it while holding the mother's key. The boy's father decided Dad made it happen, or had the power to unmake it happen and didn't. Dad does his best to prevent disaster, but he can't control everything.

I was only six years old at the time, so most of what I remember is that when we moved we couldn't bring Mom with us.

Mr. Selnick curses loud and slams the door on his way out, which makes the pheasant fall off the bookshelf, which makes Dad catch me eavesdropping.

Oops. I wave hello-there fingers at Dad.

"Come on over here next to your old man."

I join Dad at the card table.

He picks up his cup and takes a long sip like he's trying to clear his mind of the ominous vision he just had. "Mmmm. This coffee has spirit!"

I beam because Dad only uses my name as an adjective if he's pleased. "Is Mr. Selnick going to be all right?"

"I'll check on him after he's had time to calm down," Dad says. "He didn't believe me when I told him about Poppi either, but he always comes around."

Dad had predicted the birth of Mr. Selnick's daughter, Poppi, even though Mrs. Selnick swore she was long done having kids since her two other children were already grown.

"The future can be frightening. It's our responsibility to help Mr. Selnick face what lies ahead."

"He forgot his key." I pick up Mr. Selnick's house key. It's ornate and old-fashioned like a lot of things on this island. I hold it in my hand like Dad does. I rub its jagged edges with my thumb. I close my eyes tight.

Dad says the keys in our life can unlock our tomorrows. He uses people's keys to see their future selves.

Future. I flip the key in my hand over and over. Concentrate. Breathe. Imagine.

Nothing.

"I wish I'd inherited the gift." I've been holding keys every day since I turned twelve. Dad got his gift at twelve, and so did Grandmother. But I've been twelve years old for six solid months. Dad says when the gift happens, I'll feel different. I'll *know*. I'd give anything to *know* like Dad, but it seems our ancestors decided to leave me in the dark.

"Now, don't you worry," Dad says. "Keep trying. It might happen yet."

Dad is optimistic. He thinks one day I might get the gift, but he doesn't know for sure. Dad doesn't know everything. Each key decides what he should *know*. And our key won't show him anything about us—our keys have never worked for him.

Dad catches me looking at the pheasant on the floor. "You can't help others face their tomorrow if you can't face your today."

I'm not exactly sure what Dad means, but I think it has something to do with the fact that I haven't gotten rid of Sky's things.

After a few minutes of us sitting there, Dad enjoying his coffee, me having a stare-down with the pheasant, Dad blows out the candles. "Shouldn't you get started on your homework?"

"Yeah, I have some catching up to do." I haven't exactly told Dad this, but I think he knows I haven't done homework in fourteen days. That's how long Sky's been gone.

On my way out, I pick up the pheasant and then gather Sky's other toys, his bed, and his bone. I kiss the pheasant's plush beak and put it with everything else in the trash. I tie the bag and haul it outside to the can. Garbage pickup is tomorrow. Maybe if Sky's things are gone along with him, they can't hurt me anymore.

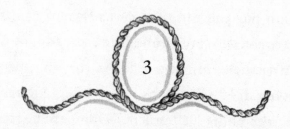

3

A DELIVERY FROM THE PAST

SCHOOL STARTS A HALF DAY LATE ON Thursdays. That's how important delivery day is on our island. It's not something you want to miss. Dad left a note saying he decided I needed my sleep, so he took the golf cart and went ahead without me. But I'd never skip delivery day. Not in a million. I'm so glad the garbage truck woke me.

I clip my walkie-talkie to my shorts and hop on my bike. I ride through the sea grass and fish smell. It's strong and wonderful.

"Dad!" I roll my bike onto the dock and park next to our golf cart. The cart's flatbed is loaded to the max with boxes, and Dad's already got Eder Mint's truck full, too. Eder is the only person on the island who owns a truck big enough to hold everything Dad orders. Dad doesn't approve of gas-guzzling, air-polluting trucks, but on delivery day he makes an exception. He says one trip in the big truck is better than a dozen with the golf cart.

"Hi, sweetheart." Dad hugs me, then hands over a box with my name on it.

"For me?" I get excited. "What did you get me?" I shake the box.

"Isn't from me," Dad says.

I smile at Eder. "Aw, Eder. You shouldn't have!"

Eder is only thirty-two, but he owns the general store, a great big house, and a ton of land. He gives fancy presents. For my birthday, I got a velvet beanbag chair softer than Sky's fur.

I jump up and down. "What is it?!"

Eder tips his hat, the one that makes him look

20

like a ship's captain. "Wasn't me, Lavender Spirit. Must be your secret admirer." He winks.

Eder calls me Lavender Spirit because I like purple so much and I'm always wearing it. Today I'm wearing my rubber-peeling purple flip-flops. They might be falling apart, but they're the best color in the rainbow.

Nector Hatterask, the only other twelve-year-old on the island, leans way over my box, being a curious snoop.

"It's got my name on it," I say, pulling the box out from under his nose. I check the return address. It's from a pet store on the mainland. Strange.

"Just making sure," Nector says. He stands on his tiptoes and scans the labels on the boxes like there's something in Eder's truck for him. He's not the only one. Other people are crowded around, too.

"More Mr. Clean?" Nector asks my dad. He's a lanky boy, and his hard elbows push me out of the way so he can get a better look.

"Watch it," I complain.

"Sorry," Nector replies, but he doesn't back up. Instead he crawls onto the truck bed. His smelly sneaker kicks into my face, almost knocking off my nose. He turns to my dad with a huge grin, totally oblivious. "Order any cereal, Mr. Holden?"

Before Dad can answer, Nector's mom marches over and yanks her son off the truck like she's sure me and Dad will bite. "Leave those dingbatters alone," she says.

Even though we've lived on Bald Island for six years, which is half my life, some people still call us dingbatters. *Dingbatters* is the word islanders use for outsiders.

The Hatterask family has been living on this island so long, people say they sprang from the soil. We'll always be dingbatters to Mrs. Hatterask. Dad says things here are slow to change, and we shouldn't be offended. So I try not to let it bother me.

But sometimes it does. We might not have lived here as long as Nector's mom, but Dad saved her children from drowning. Dad warned them about that wave, but Nector's little siblings, Yasmine and Gomez, went on the pier anyway. Dad had to jump into the ocean during a hundred-mile-an-hour hurricane and pull them out. He'd have done anything to prevent another death on his watch. When I told him I was worried he wouldn't survive, he said hard work, preparation, and a little luck were always on his side.

Dad has predicted a lot of big events that have saved lives and even some that have created new ones. He pointed out the tree that would fall through the Fishbornes' house. And not even Dr. Wade knew about Mrs. Selnick's baby. Before Dad's visions got wishy-washy and business got wonky, the phone nearly rang off the hook with people asking for readings.

But the Hatterask family has never asked for a reading. Dad says they're afraid of the future, because it's often bad for them.

Dad doesn't like people asking about his deliveries anyway. Sometimes, though, there's a label on the packaging that gives away what's inside. Like the time Dad ordered a dozen cases of Mr. Clean, and the brand was stamped in big blue letters for anyone to see. That's why Nector is asking about floor cleaner.

All those bottles of Mr. Clean started a whole bunch of rumors about the fate of the island. Why would any one person need that many bottles of soap? A flood? A disease? A supergerm? People wanted answers, and all Dad would say was he didn't *know* of a specific disaster until, finally, people stopped harassing him. But they'll never stop being curious about his piles of boxes.

Eder shifts his eyes from the rising mound inside his truck bed. He's probably worried Dad is going to flatten his tires. I think there's no way Dad can fit anything else, but then he does.

"How are you faring without that baldie?" Eder asks me.

"I miss him so much, but I'm okay," I say.

"Guess you're better off now anyway. That thing could've hurt you."

"Sky would never hurt me," I say, loud and firm, not like I'm supposed to talk to an adult, especially not Dad's best client. But when it comes to the baldies, I'll argue with anyone.

"I don't mean to upset you, Lavender Spirit. But if a baldie were in *my* house, I'd be afraid to close my eyes at night, is all. Those devilish beasts are a crime against nature."

"How can a dog be a crime?" I ask. "That doesn't even make sense."

Baldies are wild. They do what they have to do to survive. And even if he was a baldie, Sky wasn't devilish. He was a good dog. He was *my* good dog.

"Killing a young child is most certainly a crime," Mrs. Hatterask chimes in, wagging her finger at me.

"That baldie didn't mean it," I say. "He was just hungry."

A few years ago, a wild baldie knocked over a small tourist girl to get her sandwich, and she hit her head on a rock and died. Ever since, tourists haven't exactly been lining up their boats to vacation here. But islanders thinking baldies are devilish is nothing new. That particular superstition goes way back—a lot further than that little girl and her sandwich.

Mr. Fishborne, the cranky old man who runs the oyster stand, shakes his head. "Your dad told Mr. Selnick to watch out, but we should all be wary."

"Sure wish we knew more details about this terrible happening." Eder stares at Dad like he's disappointed not to know the date or time, or how fast he should drive his getaway truck. "Shouldn't whatever it is have come to pass by now? We used to be able to count on you to be right."

Mr. Fishborne slaps his leg. "It doesn't take *me* candles and incense to figure out baldies are trouble."

People standing around chuckle and nod.

I wish Sky were here so I could show everyone one more time how gentle and amazing baldies could be. But it's hopeless. Everyone hates the baldies.

At least *I* can always count on Dad.

"I do everything I can to keep my daughter and everyone else out of harm's way. My readings have been a little off lately, but I try my best. I tell you everything I *know*, and I would risk my life to protect any one of you."

People lower their eyes and get serious, because that's the kind of respect Dad deserves.

Dad hops in the golf cart and nods my way. "See you at home, sweetheart."

Eder checks the bungee cords on the boxes and fires up his engine. He waves at me as he peels out, leaving a leaky, fluorescent yellow puddle in the sand where his truck used to be.

Dad's right. Big trucks are bad for the environment.

EVEN THOUGH DAD GOT THE LAST WORD, I ride home reckless and fuming. Instead of taking the road, I dart through people's backyards, along the edge of the woods. My mystery box bounces in my bike basket like a crazed jumping bean. People didn't approve of me having a baldie for a pet. Now that he's dead, they still can't let it alone. Dad says I should always stand up for what I believe in, but he also says superstition is one of the reasons we moved here. Dad counts on people who can trust things that aren't based on science. I guess we moved to the right place.

I stare into the trees and think hard. Two baldies turning up dead? I'm surprised the island doesn't throw a party, but it makes me unsettled. I'm so busy trying to sort out what it means I don't notice the tree root that sends me over the handlebars. I hardly realize I'm off my seat until the ground whacks the air from my lungs. On my back, breathless and stunned, I stare at the sky.

No clouds. And not a bird in sight.

Bald Island may have been named after the eagles, but there are tons of other kinds of birds: whistling swans, bufflehead ducks, egrets, and white pelicans. There are over four hundred different species on our island. But I don't see a single one.

I sit up, shake off a creepy sensation, and pull the box that fell from my bicycle basket onto my lap. It's hard without a knife, but I finally manage to rip it open.

Inside is a bag of Sky's brand of kibble and a stuffed toy. I get that knocked-over-by-a-wave feeling, smacked into the sand face-first, the ocean rushing me back to shore. A shore without Sky.

He'll never again shake a stuffed toy or go to the dock with me to sit for kibble. I always liked to open his dog food right there and ask him to sit in front of everyone. People watched in awe. No one had ever seen a baldie trained to have manners. Not that it changed anyone's mind about baldies in general, but it made me proud.

Who would send me kibble and a toy for Sky? Everyone on Bald Island knows he's dead.

I pull the plastic off the toy. Its yellow-stitched eyes stare at me. Stern. As if it would disapprove of being thrown away.

Sky's pheasant.

It's exactly the same one. It's got brown furry

wings. The same green head with the white band around its neck.

But I put it in the garbage. I swear! It was hard, but I did it. I even heard the trash truck pick up our can this morning.

I smell Sky so strong I think he's here ready to catch it. I call his name and look around.

But I'm alone. Thank goodness no one's here to see me being foolish.

"Sometimes I miss you so much, buddy, I smell you. I wish you were here to play fetch." Even though he's not, I hurl the pheasant into the air.

As soon as the toy is airborne, an eagle appears. Then other birds. They fill the big blue canvas overhead as if they've come to welcome the stuffed pheasant. Another whiff of Sky fills my nostrils. If I didn't have eyes, I'd say it was dogs flying instead of birds.

As I stand to get a better look at all the birds I notice my bike. My front wheel is busted. Son of a sand fiddler! I really hit that tree root hard. Guess I deserve it for riding off the road in people's backyards. I kick the flat tire and broken rim, and the birds scatter.

All except the toy pheasant. It stares at me from where it landed in the grass. Its yellow-stitched eyes are serious and wanting. Wanting what?

Sky? I know the feeling.

I pick it up and put it in my basket. If the pheasant wants Sky, I'll take the pheasant to Sky.

A Surprise from the Past

I DIG MY TOES IN HARD, PUSHING MY BROKEN bike over heavy sand. Despite the ocean's wind, I'm sweating by the time I get to where Sky lies deep inside a sand dune.

The wind skims sand from one hill and adds it to another. The sand twirls this way and that over the beach, making a new place every day. I have to rely on instinct and the patterns of the sea grass. The grass changes, too, but slower. I wish I could put up a marker, with something on it like *Here lies Sky, the best dog a girl could have*, but the sands wouldn't hold it. Plus, I don't want anyone to know that Sky is buried.

People on this island believe that burying bodies traps souls. Lighting the body on fire sets the soul free. But on the mainland, people bury bodies in the ground all the time. Mom is buried on the mainland.

When we moved, I didn't want to leave her behind. But Dad said it wasn't practical to dig up a body after it was buried. He explained Mom is in heaven looking down on us no matter where we live. After we came to Bald Island and I found Sky sick and hurting under our house, I knew in the deepest part of my soul that Mom had sent him to me. Dad said I couldn't *know* things like that yet. But I was convinced. So I named my dog Sky, because Sky seemed like a good name for a dog from heaven.

I stand beside the spot where Sky lies beneath the sand, the spot where I found him washed up on the beach two weeks ago. His body lay in this soft curve of the dune, still as a fallen tree, his legs crumpled under him like folded branches. Was he hit by a passing boat? Why had he been in the ocean alone?

The questions didn't have answers. The only answer I had was that there wasn't anything anyone could do to save him.

So Dad and I buried him, because I couldn't bear not to have a place to visit.

"This is for you, boy." I place the pheasant on his grave. "I brought your favorite toy. Do you like it?"

The wind whips out a howl. I spin around. The howl sounded just like Sky had answered me. I look up into the clouds, where I still imagine heaven must be.

Are you up there, Sky? With Mom and Grand-mother? And all the Holden grandmothers from ages past? Dad says the women in our family are powerful holders of the Holden gift. I'm not six years old anymore, but I still believe Mom had something to do with Sky being mine. She wasn't a Holden, but she could have pulled some strings with my ancestors. She could've asked my grandmother for help.

I turn back to the dune and brush myself off. When I was sad about Mom, Sky's thick fur held my tears. Now it was best not to start them rolling.

I unclip my walkie-talkie, because I want Dad to know I'll be late. "Zookeeper calling Big Panda."

Static.

"Big Panda, are you there?"

I change channels but still get static. Like my bike, the walkie-talkie must have broken in the fall. Luck of the oyster crab has abandoned me today.

I point myself toward the Hatterasks' house. I don't want to see Mrs. Hatterask again, but her husband is the best handyman in town.

When I arrive I park my bike and check the backyard, hoping Mr. Hatterask is working there like usual.

I don't see him, so I circle back to the front to find Nector messing with my bike. He's already got the broken wheel off, ready for a new one.

Dad says Mr. Hatterask has a fixing compulsion. He can't not fix a broken thing. Maybe it runs in the family.

"You know what you're doing?" I ask Nector just to be sure.

He doesn't stop tinkering or even turn around. After a minute he stands up and wipes the gravel off his knees. "We probably don't have the right size rim, but I'll see."

"You know we get free fixings, right?" After Dad saved his kids from the wave, Mr. Hatterask gave us free fixings for life. Unlike Mrs. Hatterask, he appreciates what Dad did. "Don't think just because I'm a dingbatter, I don't know what's what."

"Shoot," Nector says. "I was hoping for a box of cereal at least." He grins wider than a clam at high tide, until he sees my face. "Day that bad? You could use some yaupon tea. There's a pot made up inside. You're welcome to a cup."

"No, thanks." Heaven forbid Mrs. Hatterask should find a dingbatter smack-dab in her own kitchen. "I think I'll just wait here."

"Suit yourself." He leaves to go to the back of the house.

Those are the most words Nector Hatterask has ever spoken to me in his life. With Sky at my side, he wouldn't even come near. Now he's climbing over our boxes, making jokes about cereal, and offering me tea at his house? I try to get over the shock.

I pace around their front yard, not sure where to wait. Everything about the Hatterask house is plain as plain can be. They don't have a porch like most people or even a set of front steps.

Mr. Hatterask could make his house the best on the island if he wanted, but since a hurricane is sure to come wreck it all, he doesn't bother. I've seen it twice myself. Storms hit their house so often people call them Hurricane Hatterasks.

I scan the yard for a comfortable spot, but the Hatterasks don't bother with lawn care either. I'm about to sit on the gravel when I notice a thin circle of metal that looks like a quarter.

I pick it up, and my whole body tingles like I've been dipped in ice. Sky's dog tag! The ocean wave of remembering knocks me back to the dunes, to Sky crumpled and still. He didn't have his tag when I found him.

What's it doing at the Hatterasks' house?

Nector comes back empty-handed. I shove Sky's tag into my pocket and try to push back the water threatening to crash out of my eyes.

"Looks like we don't have what you need," Nector says. "I'd be happy to get the part for you though. Eder's got the general store packed so tight with bikes this summer, you'd think he's expecting tourists." He laughs. "Lucky for you he's got rims and tires to spare. I can have it fixed for you by Saturday."

"Okay, thanks. My radio's also busted. You know how to fix it, too?" I unclip the walkie-talkie from my shorts and hand it to him.

Nector immediately takes it apart and gets to fiddling.

As he works, I stare into the yard near the spot where I found Sky's tag. *Were you here, Sky?* I hold his tag in my pocket and run my fingers over the etched engraving with Sky's name and my phone number.

Something rustles near the trees.

"What is it?" Nector follows my gaze.

"I thought I saw a baldie."

"Nah. They never come this side of the island. You might see them where you live, backed up against the woods like you are, but not over here." He pauses a second. "Weird that one dying in the Selnicks' yard like that. Wouldn't think they'd be at their house either. I hope they aren't getting bold."

It *is* weird. First Sky, now another baldie.

Nector's siblings, Yasmine and Gomez, run out of the house with their backpacks and a paddle-ball set.

"We're going to practice on the beach before school," Yasmine says.

Nector nods. "Be there at eleven. Don't be late because you're breaking some record." He looks at me and rolls his eyes. "You'd think they'd get bored after a while. But they can paddle for days."

Yasmine grins like this is a compliment and twirls her paddle around her hand.

Gomez gawks like he's never seen me before. "What's *she* doing here?"

"What's it look like?" Nector asks.

Gomez frowns at me, then points to a tree near their house. "Ought to take down that *Lost Dog* sign you got over there, since your dog is dead. Momma says that was the biggest waste of paper she's ever seen. No one would've gotten near enough to a baldie to tell if he was yours or not." Gomez laughs and runs to catch up with his sister.

There's nothing I can say to that, so I wait in a steamy silence for Nector to finish with my radio.

When the radio is back together again, Nector pushes the talk button and hands it to me to test.

I call Dad. "Zookeeper to Big Panda."

"Big Panda here." Dad's voice comes through loud and clear. "What's your twenty, Zookeeper?"

"My bike is broken, but I'm coming on foot from the Hatterasks' now."

"Roger that, Zookeeper. See you in ten."

"See you in ten. Zookeeper over and out."

I thank Nector.

"See you at school?" he asks.

"Yeah." On my way out, I tear down my *Lost Dog* poster. The photo of Sky makes my heart feel squeezed. Useless poster. Gomez is right. As if anyone on this island would have helped me get Sky back.

I fold the poster until it fits in my pocket because I don't want to litter. I pull out Sky's tag.

I should throw it in the trash. I make a promise to myself to do it, when something tickles my leg. I yelp and fall backward. My hands hit the tree's roots and I catch myself, but Sky's dog tag goes bouncing. "Who's there?"

I spin around, but there's nothing. My heart hammers anyway. Probably a bug, a butterfly, maybe a leaf. But when I retrieve Sky's tag, I see it. The white band. The yellow-stitched eyes.

The toy pheasant floating in midair.

I blink a few times, but the pheasant is bouncing up and down in front of me. It's bobbing in the air like it's being held by an invisible string.

But I left it on Sky's grave. If those Hatterask kids are playing a trick on me, it's a good one. I look around and in the trees, but I don't see anyone. The toy pheasant flies over the dirt road, bouncing madly. Every now and then it doubles back toward me and shakes itself. Sky's smell is everywhere. I hear him bark.

I sit stunned under the tree, unable to believe what I'm seeing. The invisible thing carrying the toy. The longer I stare, the more it takes shape.

Dog shape. Sky's shape.

I smell him. I hear him bark. I see him shake the pheasant.

"Sky? Is that you?"

5

FLOUNDERING

THE DOG HAS SKY'S FOXY TAIL. HIS BROWN
spots bold against his blond fur. His eyes. I'd know
them anywhere. Sky could command an army
with his eyes. His stare is intense.

This must be a dream. Everything is topsy-
turvy. Sky's fur, for example—it's baby soft and
young again like when he was a puppy. He's got
that puppy energy in his tail and overconfidence
in the way he stands. As if he hasn't yet learned the

world can be dangerous. But the longer I stare, the more solid he becomes. His black pupils gleam as if to say, *Follow me.*

So I do, because it's the realest dream I've ever had.

I clutch his dog tag and run after him. "Sky!" I yell. "Wait, Sky! Wait for me!" But he takes off like he's got someplace to be. Usually Sky is the one following me, not me following him.

I chase him, screaming his name, but he won't stop. I follow him across the island, running and sweating, all the way to the woods. But I can't catch him before he darts into the trees. The woods are dense and hard to navigate. I plunge in after him. For Sky, I'd step into a bed of snakes, off a cliff, down a waterfall.

I brush at my legs, hoping to scare away the insects. The mosquitoes and ticks are bad on the island, especially in the woods. I worry about getting Lyme disease. I know firsthand how awful Lyme disease can be. It was how Sky came to be mine. I found him under our house so sick he couldn't even stand up without crying, that's how painful it was for him to move. Dad figured out what was wrong with the help of the Internet, and we contacted a vet on the mainland who sent antibiotics. It seemed like a miracle the way he recovered so fast. And, well, in a way Sky's come back from the dead once already. Maybe it isn't so hard to believe he could do it again.

Branches grab at my bare arms and legs. I shove through the trees, calling his name. I tuck his tag into my pocket so I don't lose it.

But I have no idea which direction he went. I crouch down, searching for paw prints. The ground is hard and the dirt is cracked, like thirsty chapped lips. I listen carefully, but the woods are silent.

He hasn't left tracks on the ground. I don't hear the sounds of sticks breaking as he runs. It's like he disappeared into thin air.

I keep moving forward anyway. I scream his name over and over.

I scream so loud I could wake the dead.

Only I don't.

It's just me. Deep in the woods. Alone.

I DASHED INTO THE WOODS SO FRANTIC I didn't pay very good attention to where I was running. But finally I manage to find my way out and home again.

When I walk through the door, Dad jumps up from the card table. "What happened?"

"I . . ."

"I thought you said you were on the way." Dad's face goes from worried to angry.

"I was." The clock says I've been gone two hours since I radioed Dad? My detour with Sky couldn't have taken that long.

"I hate not being able to *see* anything about you. About us. I . . ." Dad drops our house key on the table—useless in this case, like Sky's *Lost Dog* posters. He takes in my sweaty face and scratched-up skin. "Where were you?"

"I saw Sky." I learned a long time ago that I can't lie to Dad. No half-truths. No leaving things out. Even if he can't see our future, he knows me too well.

Dad looks stunned. "Sky?"

I nod. "He ran off into the woods. So I chased him."

"Oh, Spirit." Dad's shoulders sag like he's incredibly sad. "You're floundering. Sky was special. I loved him, too. It broke my heart that you didn't get him back alive. But you have to face reality."

I'm still stuck on the word *floundering*, because I can swim better than any fish.

"Sky is dead." Dad pauses.

We stare at each other for what feels like a long time. The fan in the corner blows cold air down my sweaty back. I shiver.

"I know it," I whisper. As if saying it softly will make it less true.

"Then you must know that you couldn't have seen Sky."

"But I did," I insist. "Why don't you believe me?"

And he doesn't. His eyebrows hide under his hair like he can't possibly imagine what I'm talking about. "Really, Dad. It was Sky. Well, Sky as a puppy."

Dad jumps on this. "See? It couldn't have been Sky. It was just a baldie puppy that *looked* like Sky."

"They don't all look the same, Dad. Not to me. I'd recognize Sky anywhere."

"I know you would, sweetheart, but it just isn't possible. Animals can't be ghosts like people can."

What? I'm stunned. "Why not?"

Dad pauses so long, I think he'll have a good explanation, but all he says is, "They just can't."

"But how do you *know* they can't?"

"Because I've never heard of anyone seeing a ghost animal before. Our family has a long history, but nothing like this. I understand it must be frustrating not to have your gift yet, but making things up won't help it come. In fact, it will only create problems for us. You don't want people *here* to think we're charlatans do you? Please don't give them a reason." Dad puts his hand on his head like the thought of the people on the mainland who didn't understand his gift causes him pain.

"I wouldn't lie, Dad."

"I know you wouldn't. I just think maybe you saw what you wanted to see."

This doesn't entirely make sense to me, because of course I wanted to see Sky. But I didn't ask for him to be a puppy.

"You're late for school. Mrs. Dialfield already called. She's very worried. *I* was worried. You can't scare your old man like this again. It tires me out."

"You're not old, Dad."

"I'm not as young as I used to be, so promise me you won't go chasing any more baldies into the woods? Real or otherwise?"

"But, Dad—"

"Spirit." Dad says my name in his I-mean-business way.

"Okay." I nudge the fan with the end of my flip-flop. It falls over, and I have to set it upright again.

"Okay, what?"

"Okay, I promise."

"Thank you. I need to lie down. When you get home from school, wake me up."

I nod, even though it's ridiculous that Dad would still be asleep by this afternoon.

He heads up the stairs. "I'll be in the blue room."

Dad likes the blue room for naps.

"Oh, and can you drop Mrs. Borse's packages next door? She has a fit if she doesn't get them right away. You're already so late for school that two more seconds won't hurt."

"Sure," I say.

"Thank you, sweetheart."

My arms and legs are covered in sand and bramble scrapes. Before I go to school, I'll have to wash up, so I choose the red bathroom. The red bathroom is a room you can be mad in.

THE SACRED BIRD

TOWERS OF PROVISIONS COVER THE RED walls, and instead of finding bathroom regulars like toilet paper, medicine, or toothpaste, I find thirty-three boxes of macaroni and cheese (my favorite kind), ten flashlights (all with purple handles), twelve boxes of matches, enough dog food to feed Sky for years, and some yaupon tea from Mrs. Selnick. Some people barter for readings.

As infuriating as it is that Dad doesn't believe

me about Sky, I can't say he doesn't think of me. And somewhere in our house is what I actually need: witch hazel for my bug bites, a washcloth, and some soap—and we probably have all this in large supply.

I give up on finding what I need. Instead I make some yaupon tea to cure my anger. I decide going to school mad is worse than showing up hours late and covered in dirt. I gulp the tea down as quickly as I can and head out.

Of course, it's impossible to stay mad when I know that no matter what disaster may strike, I'll be eating as much mac and cheese as I want in a room lit by purple flashlights.

Even though I hate the idea that animals can't be ghosts, maybe Dad is right. It's true I thought I was dreaming at first. And they say first impressions are usually right, so I must have been.

By the time I'm standing next door on Mrs. Borse's front porch, my anger has cooled from red to pink.

I bang Mrs. Borse's knocker a few times because she's hard of hearing. "Hello? Mrs. Borse?"

I don't expect her to answer; she never opens the door when I knock. Mrs. Borse only leaves her house if she's forced to by a government-issued hurricane evacuation team. Sometimes I see her open the door real quick to grab her delivery after I'm gone. I shouldn't be nosy, but I've watched her a few times from behind some honeysuckle bushes.

I drop the boxes on her porch, but I pause when I notice that the return address on the smallest one reads *Bragg's Guns and Ammo*. I am standing there wondering what Mrs. Borse is doing ordering ammunition when the door cracks open. I straighten up so fast I almost tumble backward.

"Hi, Mrs. Borse," I croak. "I brought over your delivery from the boat."

"Come inside. Quickly, child." She yanks me into the living room and nearly slams my leg trying to get the door closed in a hurry. "I have to show you something." She snatches the top box, the one from Bragg's Guns and Ammo. "Drop the rest of those packages at the door."

Even though Mrs. Borse is inside the house with no plans to go out, she's dressed from head to toe in animal fur. As if, instead of living in a beach house, she lives in an igloo and is in danger of freezing to death.

But this is normal for Mrs. Borse. Letting me inside is not. She lets Dad in to do readings, but I have never before set one purple flip-flop through her door.

But, man oh man, have I wanted to! I've gotten enough glimpses of her through the curtains to know Mrs. Borse is the sort of person who inspires curiosity.

Her living room is a lot like her outfit. The walls are covered in deer heads and antlers, and I notice as we head up the steps that even the staircase railing looks like an animal horn. Maybe she sneaks out at night to hunt. That would explain the ammo.

As soon as we're up the stairs, she drags me

to her bedroom and whips a sheet off an enormous birdcage. Underneath is a real live bald eagle.

I gasp, because I've never seen one this close. Or in a cage.

Her head is covered in stark white feathers so clean it's like she's had a bath. "How did you get her in here?"

"What's that, child? You have to speak into my left ear. Right one's no good."

I yell the question into her left ear.

"Bird's a she? Well, I'll be."

Wait, how did I know that? I start to say I'm not sure, I just said *she* because it was the first thing that popped into my head, but Mrs. Borse accepts it like gospel.

"She came in all on her own, straight through that window."

A window by the bed is boarded up to replace the broken glass.

"She was stunned long enough for me to get her in this cage. My husband—God rest his soul—used to keep a parrot. He liked his birds to have roomy homes."

"Amazing."

"It's a thing of beauty, child. It was an eagle saved my great-grandfather. A storm got his boat, and he would have surely died. But an eagle plucked him straight out of the ocean by his belt. Carried him to this island in 1854."

"Really?" Islanders tell such crazy stories I'm never sure if I'm supposed to believe them.

" 'Course, child. Don't you believe in miracles?"

I dreamed Sky came back from the dead. It seemed like a miracle. "I believe in dreams."

"Wonderful! A dream and a miracle are sisters—practically twins. And I certainly thought I was dreaming when I saw this sacred creature crash through that window. But sacred or not, a bird coming through my window ain't natural. It's only out of respect for her maker that I didn't toss her right back out, stunned as she was, and let her die."

I nod. "That was . . . kind of you."

"But now that this bird's awake I need help. Squawks all night long, she does. Putting her in this cage right next to my bed was a terrible mistake. She's too big for me to handle by myself. And you with that baldie—a miracle if I ever saw one—trained the devil right out of him, you did."

There wasn't any devil in Sky, but I understand what she's saying, so I try not to interrupt.

"I haven't left this house since the hurricane of 2000. You wouldn't remember that. But you almost inspired me to do it. If you could just get the devil out of all of 'em." Mrs. Borse strokes her fur coat like this is a miracle so big it requires a moment to ponder.

"Now, I need you to help me with this bird. If you can train the devil out of a baldie, surely you can get this sacred creature to straighten up and fly right. She's trespassing on my property. I thank my lucky stars I thought to order myself some ammunition last week. If you can't get her out of here, I plan to shoot her."

"What? No! You can't shoot a sacred creature."

"Precisely the reason I'm asking for your help. But I'll shoot her if I have to. I get cranky without my sleep, and this bird coos a racket. Only been here a night, but she's already outworn her welcome."

The eagle's yellow beak and huge talons look breathtakingly sharp. I see why Mrs. Borse is afraid to let the bird out by herself. I hesitate.

"You have the healing touch with beasts. I saw you save that baldie."

"You mean when Sky had Lyme disease?"

She nods.

When Sky was sick, Dad said if I helped him, he wouldn't hurt me. But what about now? "What does my dad say about this?"

"You're the one I'm asking. You going to help me or not?"

I want to get Dad, but there's no way I'm leaving Mrs. Borse with the bird and the gun.

"I need this eagle out of my house." Mrs. Borse picks up the rifle resting on the wall by the bed.

I watch in horror as she loads the gun. Her eyes are icy under her warm fur hat. She cocks the rifle. "Save her or don't save her. It's up to you."

The eagle and I lock eyes. If I make a path for her, maybe she'll fly out the way she came. She doesn't want to be locked up. The solution could be that simple. "I'll need to take the boards off the window."

Mrs. Borse backs up. "Do what you have to do."

There's a hammer on the nightstand, and I use it to pry the nails out of the boards. I stack them against the wall and turn the birdcage to face the window. It's on a chest, so I'm careful not to get myself too close, because I don't want the eagle to claw me through the cage. It's a straight shot. All I have to do is open the cage door and hope the bird doesn't come at me.

"One, two, three!" I swing open the door. The cage tumbles backward, and the eagle flies out willy-nilly-crazy in every direction but the window. The objects on top of the chest go flying. Medicine bottles, a hairbrush, a framed photo of the deceased Mr. Borse holding a giant fish—everything smacks into the floor.

Mrs. Borse shrieks and points her gun. "Not my antique lamp!"

The eagle seems to enjoy the suggestion and goes straight for it, smashing the pink-flowered base into a million pieces and sending the lampshade rolling toward the bed.

Mrs. Borse takes aim at the bird, and I throw myself toward the gun. I push it up in the air, causing Mrs. Borse to fire a shot through the ceiling. The eagle goes mad and dives up and down the room, knocking things all over.

I bet I can guess how Mrs. Borse went deaf in one ear. The shot nearly broke my eardrums.

The eagle and I lock eyes again, because she's headed right at me. I stand my ground and let her come. I don't duck. I don't move. I try to use my eyes and my mind to speak to her like I always felt Sky did with me.

Home, Eagle. Fly home.

I think this command so hard I visualize the

eagle flying through the wide, empty sky, the freedom I imagine only a bird has. I picture her diving down into a big nest in a tree where her eagle family is waiting.

Inches from my head, the big bird does an abrupt about-face and spins toward the window. Out she flies, and in a flat second the chaos is over. The eagle sails into the sky.

Mrs. Borse puts down the gun and brushes her hands together. "Good riddance!"

I'M STILL SHAKEN UP FOR WHAT FEELS LIKE A long time after I leave Mrs. Borse's. I watch the sky as I walk to school. I'm looking for the eagle to make sure she finds her way home. But instead I spot a pack of baldies at the edge of the woods tucked between some people's houses. They stare at me.

I stare back, but I'm careful to make my eyes soft so I don't seem like a threat. At first, they look so much like Sky it takes my breath away. But when I look harder, it's easy to see how different they are, mangy and skinny. More ribs than fur. I brushed Sky's coat, gave him baths, and he got two meals a day, every day. Wild baldies survive on small birds and sea grass. But I still think they're beautiful. I decide right then and there that all animals are sacred. One no more than another.

THE TASTE OF FEAR

I'M SO LATE FOR SCHOOL THERE'RE ONLY thirty minutes left before the whole day is finished. But when I arrive, Mrs. Dialfield stops teaching to greet me. "Spirit's here! Isn't it wonderful?"

My classmates stare like I am the dingbatter of all dingbatters.

"Nector, show Spirit what we're working on."

There are kids of all ages in our class, so

Mrs. Dialfield tries to have us all on the same topic but at different levels. Nector and I are the only ones doing the exact same thing.

When I sit down, Nector bursts out words like a whale holding in the ocean. "I'm sorry about my family this morning. I wanted to apologize earlier about my mom, then Gomez was rude, and I—"

"Don't worry about it," I say.

He breathes a sigh of relief and pushes over his drawing of soil sections so I can see what we're learning. His drawing has a bunch of lines and labels sticking out in every direction. "I never realized dirt was so complicated," he says. "Did you?"

I shake my head and think about how Nector's family has been on this island so long, people say they sprang from the soil. Like all those living organisms under our feet could multiply into the skinny brown boy next to me. I don't think this is literally true, but sometimes it's hard to know what to believe.

Gomez and Yasmine sit with the ten- and eleven-year-olds. Gomez was four and Yasmine five when the wave hit the pier.

"Your mom should be grateful we live here," I say suddenly, because I can't help myself and, well, she really should be. "Not everyone is lucky enough to have the people they love still alive."

"She's grateful. She's just . . ." Nector dog-ears the page in our science book. He keeps folding it back and forth, not finishing his sentence.

I'm afraid he's going to make that tiny piece fall off, and Mrs. Dialfield will have more reasons to be disappointed, us having ripped a textbook other kids for years to come need to use. But I'm so curious about what he's going to say, I let it slide. "She's just what?" I prompt.

"Worried. She doesn't want anything else to fret about." The tiny piece Nector's been creasing falls off. He stares at it in his hand like he had no idea that would happen. "Your dad orders all those supplies. Every time Mom sees them, she gets nervous."

"Oh." I guess having your house knocked down in every storm would be enough to worry about.

"We never have more than a day's worth of food. Mom doesn't like to keep much because the storm always takes it."

"If there's a disaster and you need something, we have extra," I offer. "Or even if there isn't and you need something . . . assuming I can find it. Our house is kind of a mess."

"Thanks." Nector smiles. He tries to fit the tiny triangle, the torn piece of textbook page, back into place, but without tape it'll never stick.

Finally he gives up and slides the book over so I can begin reading. I do, but eventually I get to the part about how what's buried in the earth decomposes, and it's hard not to be sad about Mom and Sky.

Inside my pocket I rub Sky's dog tag the same way I used to rub his fur if I was nervous or needed to think hard.

A flash. A flutter. Like before, only this time outside the window, Sky's blond fur and big brown spots. Sky's paws on the window glass. My heart races, and my brain screams, *It's him! It's really Sky!*

But I resist the urge to jump out of my seat and chase him, because I'm dreaming. I have to be. Dreaming and its sister, a miracle that can never be.

I close my eyes, then reopen them.

Sky doesn't budge. Once he has my attention, he takes his paws off the window and sits. It took me months to train him to sit politely like that.

He waits, patient. His eyes lock onto mine. *Follow me,* they say.

When I don't, he repositions himself into what looks like a four-legged foot stomp. *Follow me.*

I bury my nose in my textbook and try to concentrate. This is science, and if I have any hope of helping more animals, maybe being a vet someday, I have to stop missing assignments. Stop daydreaming and wishing for miracles. Stop seeing what I want to see. Dr. Wade is the only doctor on the island, and he doesn't know a lick about animals. When Sky was a puppy and we found him sick, Dr. Wade just wiggled his gray eyebrows and shrugged. He wouldn't even come look at him.

It felt great to help the eagle. It would feel great to help more animals.

But my eyes wander back to the window—to Sky, clearer than any science book. I lean over to Nector.

He jumps a little, like he forgot I was there.

"Do you see that?" I point to where Sky waits for me in the grass.

"See what?" Nector's stare is blank.

I'm the only one who sees a dog come back to life.

Dad was right. I'm floundering.

I rub Sky's tag to calm down, but it doesn't work. It's hard to be calm when you realize you're crazier than trigger-happy Mrs. Borse.

After school, I wait until all my classmates leave, then I approach Mrs. Dialfield. She is making tea.

"Would you like some?" Mrs. Dialfield asks, her thin arm already reaching for a second mug.

"What kind is it?"

"What kind does it smell like?"

Mrs. Dialfield can't smell or taste things, so I inhale the sweet honey air for her. But underneath the sweet smell is a real stink. Yaupon tea reeks like a rotten holly bush, and it tastes bad, too. You're only supposed to drink it if you're angry, like I was this morning when Dad didn't believe me about seeing Sky. But Mrs. Dialfield has lived on this island less than a year, so maybe she doesn't know that.

"It smells sweet, like yaupon tea." I lie about the smell, because it doesn't seem nice to sour things for Mrs. Dialfield. "Are you angry?" I ask.

Instead of answering, she hugs me. I can feel her bones. She might be thinner than the baldies. It occurs to me that I've never seen her angry, though she must have lots of reasons to be mad.

After a minute she lets me go and smiles, calm and warm like always. The smile she gives even when kids like me don't turn in their assignments. "I'm not angry. I haven't said this to you yet, but I want to now: I'm sorry for your loss."

It's the first time anyone's been sorry about me losing Sky, and it feels right.

"When I lost the ability to taste, people said things that made me furious. *You're lucky to be alive. You can hear and see, and those are the important senses. Life is more than food. You'll find something else you love.* I needed an entire island to contain my rage. Do you know even though I couldn't taste a bite of food, I could taste my anger?"

"Really? What did it taste like?" I ask.

"Fear."

This doesn't really help, since I'm not sure what fear tastes like either, but eating anger seems like an odd thing to do anyway.

She keeps talking. "So I picked up and moved here, and then I waited to die."

"You can't die," I say.

"Your dad is such a blessing. He saw the good coming in my life when I could see none. Today there's a girl in front of me with an imagination so strong, her dog will never die."

"I see him. His ghost," I whisper, because Sky is

still waiting for me in the grass, and I figure crazy people who see ghost animals need help. "But I know it's not possible."

"Lots of impossible things happen on this island. I thought I'd never cook again, but when I see you sad and hurting, I want to make a feast." She holds out her arms like she's showing me a long table filled with food.

Before she got cancer, Mrs. Dialfield used to be a famous chef in New York. She says she can't cook professionally anymore because a chef has to be able to taste the food to know if it's good. Thankfully she didn't lose her vocal cords, or she couldn't be our teacher. I can't say if she was a good chef or not, but she's a really good teacher.

"I like cookies," I suggest.

She laughs. "Honeysuckles are nice this time of year. What about honeysuckle sorbet? Last day of school is next week. Could be a great way to celebrate."

I wrinkle my nose. "What's a sorbet?"

She laughs again. "You'll see."

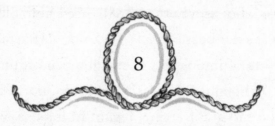

POOR MR. SELNICK

ON SATURDAY I STOP BY THE HATTERASKS' TO pick up my bike. Mr. Hatterask and Mr. Selnick are sitting in the gravel yard in short beach chairs.

"Is Nector home?" I ask Mr. Hatterask. "He was fixing my bike for me."

"The kids went to the beach," Mr. Hatterask says. "But it's ready for you in the backyard."

A pang of sadness hits that Nector didn't invite me, even though no Hatterask has ever invited me anywhere before. Why would they start now? I shake it off. Saturdays are lonelier without Sky, is all. *Where are you, buddy?* I look to the Hatterasks' trees again, hoping to catch a glimpse of him. If Mrs. Dialfield thinks it's possible for Sky to be a ghost, then maybe I'm not crazy. Maybe like everyone else on this island, Dad just doesn't realize the baldies are special.

"Spirit, help me up, will you?" Mr. Selnick reaches his big arms toward me.

The chair is so low to the ground, I can't see how a man his size got down there. When I pull him up, I see the chair is the kind good for dipping your legs in the ocean. The plastic strips probably used to be red, but the sun has faded them ghost white.

Instead of using these awful beach chairs, Mr. Hatterask should build some nice benches. He could do it easy. Maybe if he nailed them down, a hurricane wouldn't get them.

"I'm happy to make you another key if you think that'll help," Mr. Hatterask says to Mr.

Selnick. He grabs Mr. Selnick's arm to help steady him. The big guy seems a bit wobbly on his feet.

"Girl's father has never been wrong before." Mr. Selnick nods in my direction. "I hate to admit it, but I'm sure he's right."

Just like Dad predicted, Mr. Selnick has come around.

He shakes his head. "Knows everything, that man."

Not everything. Dad didn't know that Sky and Mom were going to die. Or that I'd see Sky's ghost.

"He certainly doesn't know everything," Mr. Hatterask says, like he read my mind. "Even Mint says so these days, and you know how addicted Eder is to knowing every little thing."

"My dad's been distracted lately, is all. He knows a lot of things. Had a fine vision the other day for Mr. Selnick. Real specific."

"He knows enough for me," Mr. Selnick says.

I'm so glad to see Mr. Selnick's loyalty is back, even when the future is bad news.

I'm about to head to the back of the house when Eder Mint's truck pulls up. What happened to his loyalty? I want to ask him why he hasn't been in for a reading in a while, but Dad wouldn't like it. He thinks it's important people come to him by their own will.

"Selnick, glad I caught you," Eder says. "Has anything—"

Mr. Selnick shakes his head. "Nothing so far."

Eder shakes his head, too. "If we don't watch out, baldies are going to be the death of us all sooner or later."

"Now wait a minute." Mr. Selnick holds up a finger. "No one said anything about me dying. It's something terrible, no doubt, but..." The big man wobbles again like he's too weak to keep standing.

"Be careful now or you'll fall over," Eder says. He looks thoughtful. "Sure hope you wore gloves when you moved that baldie to the beach to burn him."

Mr. Selnick looks surprised. "I didn't."

Eder's eyes fill with worry. "You could get sick."

Mr. Selnick wobbles again to the right. Mr. Hatterask tries to catch him, but suddenly Mr. Selnick wobbles left. Eder grabs for his arm and misses.

I grab for the other arm. But Mr. Selnick pitches forward before any of us can steady him and lands in a heap at my feet.

I scramble to help him back upright. His face is colorless and slick with sweat. It's pale, not black like Dad said it would be. His shirt isn't the blue plaid one Dad predicted either. "He's not wearing the right shirt," I say.

But Mr. Selnick groans like he's in terrible pain.

I frown at Eder. "The baldies don't make people sick. Why would you think that?"

Eder ignores me. "You need to see the doctor, Selnick." He nods at Mr. Hatterask. "I'll take him."

Eder and Mr. Hatterask carry Mr. Selnick to the truck. I insist on helping. I'm little, but I'm strong from swimming.

Mr. Hatterask says, "He's burning up. Get him a cold washcloth, will you?"

I rush into the house. The walls are wide and blank, and the only furniture looks lightweight and temporary. The Hatterasks' house is as plain and empty on the inside as it is on the outside. I almost trip on a piece of wood coming out of the floor. I realize the boards aren't nailed down. I pause and wonder for a moment if Mr. Hatterask forgot to secure them the last time he rebuilt after a hurricane, but when I pull on one, it rises up like the floor itself is a trapdoor.

"What are you doing?" Mrs. Hatterask walks toward me and pushes the floorboards back into place. "Weather report didn't say a thing about a storm today."

"Sorry, I . . ."

Her face is forbidding. "If you or your dad know different, don't you dare tell me. I was all set to have a pleasant afternoon, and I intend to keep it that way."

"I won't," I promise. But if Dad had a vision of

another hurricane, I don't understand why she wouldn't want to know.

She nods. "Good. Best run along, then."

She doesn't have to tell me twice. I scramble out of there, wondering how I'm going to explain not having a washcloth, but when I get outside Eder's big truck is gone.

THE KEY TO SKY

EARLY SUNDAY MORNING I RIDE MY BIKE over the whole island looking for Sky. But he's vanished like the ghost that he is. I look for him outside the school windows, around the Hatterasks' trees where I saw him before, and along the edges of the woods. But I can't find him anywhere.

When I get home and put my key in the front door, I get so nauseous I almost puke on the doorstep. Maybe I caught what made Mr. Selnick so sick yesterday. Stomach viruses sweep the island every now and then.

"Dad?" He doesn't answer. I muster the strength to call again. "Dad? Are you home? I'm back from my bike ride, and I'm not feeling so great."

Maybe he's out giving a reading. But I find a long Dad-shaped mound in the blue room under the cornflower comforter.

"Dad?" I shake him awake. "You slept all morning . . . again?" I'd been out for several hours. "You might have the stomach bug, too," I say.

Dad's been tired for a few months, but not sleeping-all-day-every-day tired. He lowers his legs to the floor with such effort I wonder if he pulled his back unloading all those boxes on Thursday. "What day is it?" He stares up at me groggy-eyed and confused, like instead of taking a nap, he traveled to another dimension.

"Sunday." I help him out of bed. "Are you sick?"

"We have to try a reading," he says. "Are you ready?"

"Ready for what? Dad, are you talking in your sleep?" A creepy feeling snakes up my spine.

"Mr. Selnick," he says. "Help me up. We're going to visit Mr. Selnick."

Dad walks to the Selnicks' house with his arm across my shoulder—too weak to stand up straight and too delirious to make much sense.

"Please let me get Dr. Wade," I beg. "I think you have a terrible fever."

But Dad shakes his head.

We knock on the Selnicks' door, and Poppi answers wearing a diaper and a cartoon T-shirt. "GeePa!"

Poppi can't say *godfather* yet. She puts her arms in the air toward Dad.

Dad kisses the top of Poppi's forehead, but he doesn't pick her up and throw her in the air like usual. He stumbles into the house. "Jolie?" he shouts.

"Back here," Mrs. Selnick answers.

Dad stops to lean on the wall for a moment like shouting took all the energy he had left. His face is as white as the paint.

"Please let me get the doctor," I insist. But when we get inside the Selnicks' bedroom, I see the doctor is already here.

Dad falls into a chair by the window and waves me toward the bed, where Mr. Selnick lies pale and still, his wife at his side. He looks like a blowfish slowly deflating.

"What's wrong with him?" I ask Dr. Wade.

"Not sure, to be honest," the doctor says.

"It's the devil," Mrs. Selnick whispers. "Devil got him when he touched that baldie."

"Well, it *is* mysterious," Dr. Wade agrees. "I'll give you that. I've never seen anything quite like it."

Dad slumps over in the chair, like even sitting up is too much.

"Dad? Are you okay?"

Dr. Wade rushes over. He clucks his tongue. "Looks like this thing is contagious. Shame it's not responding faster to the medication. Something this bad has the potential to wipe out the island."

Dad shakes his head in protest, but he looks so sick I worry Dr. Wade is right.

Fear rushes up my throat. Bitter. Fear tastes bitter.

"Ask for the Selnicks' key," Dad urges me.

Normally before Dad can give a reading the person needs to ask him for it, so I'm not sure why Dad wants Mr. Selnick's key. But Mrs. Selnick hands it to me without question.

I pass it to Dad, but he refuses and pushes it toward me. "You," he whispers.

"Me?" I drop the Selnicks' key, even though Dad didn't try to take it, and it never left my hand. When I pick it up, I realize why. It's hot. Not burn-you-up metal-pot-handle hot, but just hot enough to be slightly uncomfortable. "Was it lying in the sun?" I ask.

"Been here in Mr. Selnick's pants pocket," Mrs. Selnick says.

Dad nods enthusiastically like the fact that it's hot means I'll be able to glean something from it. Know the future. Cure the sick. Dr. Wade and the Selnick family watch me hopefully. Like I am a miracle worker instead of a giftless twelve-year-old girl. Having predicted Poppi, Dad has set their expectations high.

"Dad, please, it's you the Selnicks need, not me." Dad has been giving readings for three decades. Even if he's sick and a tad rusty, all he has to do is take the key, and he'll *know* a lot more than I ever could.

Dad shakes his head. "The power has moved on."

Moved? Moved where?

"You," Dad whispers again, like knowing the future is as simple as brown-bagging oatmeal and eggs at the general store.

I flip the key in my hand. Rub its jagged edges. Concentrate. On what? How can I know the answer if I don't know the question?

"But you already gave Mr. Selnick a reading," I argue. "Remember the fire, Mr. Selnick saying, *We should've left the island*?"

Dad looks surprised. "I didn't say anything about a fire."

"What fire?" Mrs. Selnick pats the bed blankets in a panic, like flames are licking at her husband's fingertips—as if the saying of a thing pops it into being. Maybe this is how Poppi got her name.

"Sorry. I must have made that up. I thought Dad said there would be a fire. Maybe I thought it because I smell something burning." I turn to Mrs. Selnick. "Did you leave the stove on?"

"Haven't cooked at all today. People been so kind, bringin' over food. Mrs. Fishborne brought over oyster stew, and Mrs. Dialfield made up some—"

"So there's going to be a fire," Dad interrupts as if it's a statement of fact. "That makes sense." He looks thoughtful, like he's recalling the vision. "His face was smudged black . . . Could have been ash."

"I don't know the future, Dad. I do smell something burning though." I sniff the air again and hand the Selnicks' key back.

Dr. Wade and the Selnicks watch me intently.

"Well, I don't know. Maybe not. I don't smell it

now. I'm sorry I . . ." For comfort, I tuck my free hand in my pocket and find Sky's dog tag, there from the last time I wore these shorts. Then, behind Dad's head outside the Selnicks' window, I see Sky, wagging his tail and shaking the toy pheasant like he's happy to see me.

The dog tag! When I touch it, Sky appears.

Sky drops the pheasant. Barks. Raises his rear end in the air. Dog language for *Want to play?*

As soon as I let go of Sky's tag, he's gone. *Poof.* Touch the tag, he appears. Release it, he disappears. I try this a few times, and it continues to work. Appear. Disappear. Appear. Disappear.

Dad follows my gaze out the window. "What is it? What do you see?"

The Selnicks keep a horse in their backyard— the only horse on the island. He snorts.

Dad looks disappointed, like he thinks I'm horse-gazing instead of helping poor Mr. Selnick. How can I tell him the ghost of my dead dog wants to play, especially when he's so sure animals can't be ghosts? I touch and release Sky's dog tag again.

Appear.

Disappear.

Appear.

Disappear.

Well, if Sky isn't real, at least my imagination has an on/off switch.

10

BALDIE LEGEND

ON THE WAY HOME FROM THE SELNICKS', DAD stops to throw up in Mrs. Borse's bushes, and when I put my key into our door, I feel like puking, too. It has to be a stomach bug.

But Dad says, "It's not a bug. This is what happens when the gift passes from one generation to the next."

My heart pounds like when the undertow catches me off guard, pulls me out too far, makes me lose my footing. "Why didn't you tell me that we'd get sick—that you'd lose your gift?"

"I didn't want to worry you."

"If I'm supposed to have the gift, why didn't I see anything when I held Mr. Selnick's key?" Darkness, as if I were at the beach on a moonless night, that's all I saw.

"It'll come," Dad says. "We'll keep trying." He sits at the table where he gives readings, like he can't make it any farther. "If you get sick when you touch a key, or it feels warm, it's the key's way of warning you something powerful is coming. It's . . ." Dad pauses like he's thinking of how to explain it. "It's the key's way of asking us to have courage. We must help others face what lies ahead, but first we must face ourselves."

"Do you always feel sick when you touch a key?"

Dad shakes his head. "It's the worst when you're learning. When I was your age, the first time, I threw up in your grandmother's good chowder pot." He laughs. "Boy, was she furious!

After that I learned to run outside when I felt sick."

"How long did it take before you learned to use your gift?"

"Don't worry, sweetheart. We'll both feel better soon." He puts a heavy hand on mine. "I'm tired. I've got to rest now."

I want to ask Dad a million more questions. I want him to teach me so I can help us not to be sick. Most of all, I want to ask him if it's possible I caught a different gift. The kind that involves a ghost dog.

But Dad hugs me tight and whispers, "I know you have the courage to face what lies ahead. I will be so proud." Then he stumbles back into the blue bedroom to sleep.

I'm wondering why Dad used the future tense, like when he has a vision, like he knows for sure I'll do something to be proud of, when the phone rings. It's Mrs. Borse. I assume she wants Dad—to ask for a reading or to complain about the throw-up in her bushes—but it turns out she wants me. Something flew through the window. Again.

Maybe it's a Pegasus. At this point, I'd believe anything. The world seems upside down and inside out.

"It's something that belongs to you," she says.

"Can you bring it over?"

"Don't be smart with me," Mrs. Borse warns.

She's right, of course. I know she won't leave her house to come over. But I figured it wouldn't hurt to ask. "Okay, I'll be right there." I leave the door unlocked so I don't have to touch my key and get a jolt of nausea.

MRS. BORSE OPENS THE DOOR SO THERE'S JUST a sliver of space to squeeze in. I have to flatten myself like a sheet of cardboard. It's eighty degrees in June, but she is still dressed head to toe in fur. She even has one of those Russian-looking hats with the earflaps.

"Have a seat, and I'll get what's yours."

I sit on her couch in the center of the severed animal heads, and the smell of fur and skin shoots up my nose like a bullet. "Did you kill these animals yourself?" I ask.

She disappears up the stairs. "If you're talking to me, child, I can't hear you. You'll have to wait till I come down so you can talk into my good ear."

I wait with my bodiless friends, and an anger rises within me. If I were dead, I wouldn't want my head on a wall.

"Couldn't sleep a wink last night." Mrs. Borse's voice trails down. "Blasted baldies howling for hours. If my husband were alive, he'd shoot them all. Make me a new fur coat."

I stand up. "I don't care what you have of mine—you can keep it." The only thing I want back is Sky, and I already have the key to getting him.

"I can't hear you, child," Mrs. Borse calls.

The urge to bolt is hurricane-strong, but I force

myself to wait for her to come down the stairs. When she does, I say, "If you can't hear me, how can you hear the baldies?"

"Got one good ear."

"Well, sleep on it, then, so you can't hear them." It comes out mean and as angry as I feel, loud enough for her to hear it on the first try. When I see her surprise, my fury curls back.

"Child . . ." She pauses.

"I'm sorry, but those animals." I point to the wall. "They're dead, and their heads are—"

She swings her own furry head around as if she's forgotten what's on the walls. "You're not one of those vegetarians are you?" She drawls the word *vegetarian* like it's foreign and hard to pronounce.

I shake my head.

One side of Mrs. Borse's grumpy face turns into an almost smile, and she slaps my back. "Good."

I've won her approval, but it doesn't feel good. A swirl of confusing emotions twists inside me, but I can't seem to lay them straight. Finally I say, "The baldies aren't your enemy."

"It's easy to be brave, child, when you don't know any better. You don't understand about the baldies." Mrs. Borse shudders like the thought of them, even in all her fur, gives her a chill. "You didn't grow up hearing their history like I did, because you aren't from around here. But maybe it's time someone told you a thing or two about those devil creatures." She pushes me back onto the couch and gets herself comfortable like we'll be there awhile. "You know what legends are?"

"Stories that aren't real?" I guess.

"Legends are the realest kind of stories, told over and over by people for generations. My grandfathers and grandmothers told my mother and father, and they told me, and now I'll tell you."

"Okay," I say, skeptical. When I first got Sky, kids tried to tell me some of these stories about the baldies, but I thought they were making fun of me, so I didn't listen.

Mrs. Borse settles further into the couch, and I lean in despite myself.

"My great-great-grandmother of many ages ago was sick with smallpox. Late one night, she was called from her sleep by a howl in the wind. *Come to me,* the howl said, *and you will be cured of this illness that plagues you.*" Mrs. Borse slaps her chest. "She was very sick, but I come from strong stock. And my great-great-grandmother wanted more than anything to be well again, so she followed the howl into the depths of the darkness. *I am here!* she cried. *Make me well, as you promised!* But the howl was a devil baldie, hiding in the shadows. All of my great-great-grandmother's evil deeds, every sin from her entire life, flashed before her eyes, and she knew she had been tricked. *No, please,* she cried. *I will be good, I promise. Please let me go.* But the devil baldie leaped out"—Mrs. Borse throws her hands in the air—"and ate her."

I wait a bit, because I'm not sure the story is finished, but Mrs. Borse doesn't go on. She watches me carefully.

Finally, I say, "But how could your great-great-grandmother tell anyone what happened to her if she was dead?"

"Well . . ." Mrs. Borse frowns and scratches under her hat. "Huh. You ask too many questions, child. I was so frightened when my grandfather told me that story the first time, I shrieked and got a whuppin'! It didn't scare you?"

I shake my head.

"My mind isn't what it used to be. Maybe I'll tell you another one sometime, if I can remember how it goes."

"There are more?"

"Oh, there're plenty. There's the one with the man and the watch, the one with the woman and the lighthouse, the one with the sailor and the moon. Nearly every family on this island has a history they can tell you about the baldies."

"They sound like ghost stories."

"They're scary. That's for sure."

"Ghost stories aren't real though," I say, but even as I do, I think of Sky.

"Well, this is real enough and strange, too. It belongs to you." She hands me a piece of paper.

"This is what flew in through the window?"

She nods.

It's the packing slip from my mainland pet store order, listing Sky's dog food and the pheasant. Also printed in a bordered box, labeled *Gift Note*, it says:

> *Great gifts require great talents*
> *Great talents require great sacrifice*
> *Great sacrifices require great time*
> *We hope you accept and enjoy*
> *The great gift*
> *Granted you by the Greats*

"Did you type this on here?" I show her the printed message.

"Got better things to do than keep up with gift giving. If I missed your birthday, I'm sorry."

She rises, makes a sliver in the door, and pushes me toward it. "You go on now, okay? It's time for my nap."

Outside, I study the lines on the packing slip. My birthday was six months ago. Who would bother to send a gift so late? And I can't think of anyone who would send dog food even on the right day. Never mind write such a weird message.

Great gifts require great talents

Who would think dog food and a stuffed pheasant were *great* gifts? Not that I don't appreciate them, but it seems like whoever sent this might be talking about more than what was in the box.

I have more questions than answers. Who are the Greats? What great talents? And then I want to know.

Sky. Are you my great gift?

11

MY GREAT GIFT

SINCE I LEFT OUR DOOR UNLOCKED, I FEEL
fine stepping inside the house. Dad's right about
my sickness being connected to my key. I check on
him to see if he feels better, but he has the blanket
pulled over his head. I pull the curtains closed so
the sun won't be in his eyes if he throws off the
covers. Then I eat a peanut butter and jelly sandwich and tiptoe to his office to use the computer.

The computer is buried in the back of the room

behind a pile of supplies. Dad has been stockpiling since we moved here, preparing not only for every disaster he couldn't see but also, I realize, for one he could: losing his power and his income. I'm relieved to see we can eat for a while. Jobs are hard to come by on an island this small, and it might take a long time for me to learn to use my power well enough to make money.

I turn on the computer and sit on the stack of boxes Dad uses for a chair. I enter the number from the slip to look up my delivery order.

The gift note is printed on the computer screen, along with the items ordered, just like it is on the paper in my hand. If Mrs. Borse typed the message, she also hacked into this order site. It seems like a lot of trouble for her to go to, and I'm pretty sure Mrs. Borse doesn't even own a computer, since Dad helps her place her orders. I think the order was placed by someone else. Someone who wanted Sky to have food and a toy in the afterlife. Which is pretty nice if you think about it.

I phone the number on the slip, and after some

annoying music, finally I'm connected to a live human.

"Yes, I'm trying to see who placed an order I received."

"Order number?"

I give him the number.

"Your name, please."

"Spirit Holden."

"Thank you, Ms. Holden. This order was placed by Holden Spirit."

"You mean Spirit Holden?"

"Yes," the man on the line says back.

"But I didn't place the order."

"Are you Holden Spirit?"

"No, I'm Spirit Holden."

"Yes."

"Yes?"

"Yes, Holden Spirits placed the order."

"Spirits? Did you say *Spirits* with an *s*?"

"Yes."

"Can you spell it, please?" I grab a piece of paper and a pen.

When the man finishes spelling, I've written *Holden Spirits.*

I stare at the words, and then I reread the gift note on the packing slip.

Holden Spirits.

The Greats.

My ancestors?

Great-grandfathers and great-grandmothers? They're Holden Spirits. The Holden Spirits who hold the family gift.

I hang up the phone. I'm sweaty and my head is spinning. I go to the kitchen and stick my head in the freezer.

After a minute, I can think clearly again.

Maybe I should hold my key until it tells me why all this is happening. Dad says even though he can't *know* things with his own key, Grandmother could. Maybe I can, too. Great gifts require great time. Maybe great gifts also require great practice. If I have the power inside me somewhere, maybe it's time to draw it out.

I go outside, because I don't want to get sick in

the house, and then I take the key from my pocket. The heavy metal lies still in my palm until a jolt of nausea strikes powerful enough to make me drop it. It thuds onto the porch right near a crack, almost falling under the house. I pick it up and try again—this time on the dirt road, where it'll be safe even in my butterfingers. I hold on until I throw up.

Despite seeing my peanut butter and jelly sandwich in liquid form on the road, I don't *see* anything. I don't *know*.

Maybe I'm like Dad. Maybe I have to hold someone else's key to *know*. No one's asked me to do a reading, so I give up on this idea in favor of seeing something I know I can. Sky. I rub his tag, and he appears, his tail wagging so hard his whole body shakes.

"If you're my gift, are you here to help me do readings, buddy? Do you know the future?"

He has the stuffed pheasant in his mouth. He drops it and grins.

"You think that's funny, huh?"

Sky picks up the toy bird again and runs away with it, wanting me to chase him.

"Come back, Sky! I don't feel like playing!" I'm still a little queasy.

He stands for a minute, waiting for me to come, but when I don't he runs back to me.

I try to pet him, to say *Good dog,* but my hand waves through him. Like he's a ray of sunlight.

I can touch the pheasant but not Sky. They look equally three-dimensional, but my hand continues to slide through Sky whenever I try to pat his puppy head. He's young and healthy. His fur looks so soft. It's hard to believe he isn't real. Or real in the way he once was. I'm disappointed. I want to hug him close. Feel him lick my face. But it's pretty exciting that he's here now. That it's me and Sky again. Together. Like it should be.

I run toward the house to get the kibble from the delivery box. If I can't pet him, maybe I can reward him with a treat. If the Holden ancestors sent it, I wonder if there's also something special about the bag of kibble. For a piece of kibble, will Sky tell me the future?

I figure Sky will follow me in the house like he usually does, but as soon as I hit the porch, he stops short. He sits, patient.

"Come," I command.

He paces back and forth in front of the steps like he can't go any farther.

"Come, boy. Come."

More pacing.

"Stay," I say instead, putting up my hand.

He waits while I run inside.

I come back out with the kibble. Sky stands up and wags his tail. He knows he's about to get fed. I hold a piece of kibble in one hand, always the dog tag in the other, and make him sit again. He obeys. But when I hand him the kibble, it falls on the ground like it didn't even touch his lips.

Sky pushes it with his nose, tries to bite it, but the kibble doesn't move an inch. He stares up at me as if he's asking, too. Why isn't the kibble magic like the pheasant?

"I'm sorry, boy. Maybe ghost dogs don't need to eat. I don't have all the answers." I fold the bag of kibble and leave it on the porch.

Sky runs off toward the beach. A swim seems like a great idea, so this time I follow.

Sky can run a lot faster than I can, even when I'm not feeling queasy, so he stops every now and then and looks back—waits for me to catch up.

Such a good dog. My heart soars. It's me and Sky. Off to the beach. Together again.

A DEATH AT SUNSET

I FOLLOW SKY TO THE BEACH WHERE THE OLD
pier once stood. Yasmine and Gomez knock their
pink rubber ball between the paddles like it
doesn't bother them they nearly died in this spot.
Gomez catches sight of me and misses the ball.

"You dummy!" Yasmine yells. She scoops up a
crab from the sand. It dangles from her hand, and
she chases her brother with it. They run this way
and that over the sand. She catches up to him, and

Gomez snatches the crab away and throws it at her. She screams bloody murder.

I look down and Sky is tugging at my shorts, or trying to anyway. I can't feel him. I can only see. He wants to pull me toward Yasmine and Gomez, like he sees that pink rubber ball and thinks it looks fun. "No," I say. "I don't want to play with them."

He keeps trying to tug me toward the ball.

"Let's go swimming!" I say. I kick off my shoes and run for the ocean, clothes and all.

Sky stands on the beach, not following. He stares at the Hatterask kids.

"Come, boy. You love swimming," I insist.

Finally Sky follows me into the ocean. He doesn't make a splash, so I make one big enough for both of us. I don't care that Yasmine and Gomez will think I've lost my mind. I love swimming with Sky.

It's still hard to believe he would go swimming alone. "Why'd you do it?" I ask him. But he just keeps looking back at Yasmine and Gomez like they have a juicy treat he can't resist.

"Ignore them," I say firmly. I crawl into the waves, determined to get as far away as possible. I squeeze Sky's dog tag tight in my hand, willing him to come. Reluctantly, he follows.

We swim way out, diving under the waves until we get to where it's calm and still, like a lake. We pass where the pier would have ended, where Yasmine's screeches are too far to reach us.

I flip onto my back and float. I relax, but I'm careful not to lose my grip on Sky's tag. The cool water curls around my hair and into my clothes. Sky dog-paddles around me. His wet-dog odor is strong. But he doesn't look wet, and his body doesn't make waves. I don't need the raft. I don't have to worry he'll get tired and drown.

The sun is setting. The red and orange light up the ocean like a fire. The clouds turn into purple silhouettes. They float above like a moving quilt. It's a perfect moment.

So perfect it takes me a few minutes before I hear Sky's barking. My head rests deep in its water pillow. Even in the stillness, the ocean laps noisily in my ears. When I finally hear, I know Sky's been barking awhile, because his jaw strains open so wide I can see the back of his throat. It's his guard-dog-danger bark.

I sit up in the water so fast I nearly drink in the whole ocean. I cough it up, but Sky's left me, like he just couldn't wait any longer for me to get a clue. He swims to shore as if the red and orange waves are flames he must escape. I follow, one hand a tight fist over Sky's tag. My arms and legs burn. I haven't swum this fast, well, ever. I'm not sure if we're running from something or toward it, but the water is in my way. The water is between me and Sky. I work hard to close the gap.

Sky hears better than me, always could. But as I stand up in the shallow waves, I hear it, too. Shrieking. Bloody murder for real.

The undertow has pulled me far away from where the Hatterask kids were playing. I tear down the beach after Sky toward them. Yasmine and Gomez wave their arms in the air, jumping up and down like they're trying to flag a boat in the ocean far away. Unless they can see Sky bounding toward them, the boat must be me.

Sky gets to them before I do, and the three of them look like they are doing some kind of dance together. I don't think they can see Sky, but it's eerie the circle the three of them make. But not as eerie as what's in its center. A crumpled heap of wet fur, a wet-dog smell so pungent there's no doubt it's real.

Sky howls the howl of the dead. A deep rumbling wail of sadness.

Lifeless. The other baldie looks like Sky did. I marvel that he lies only a few sand dunes away from Sky's grave. As if he knew this was a baldie graveyard.

"Scared the creepers out of us!" Yasmine says, her voice high-pitched and breathless. "I thought it was alive."

How she could ever think this poor crumpled dog was alive is beyond me. That she would *truly* be scared if he were? Even more unimaginable.

"Do you have a lighter?" Gomez asks. "We could drag him to the water. Send him out."

"We should bury him," I say.

They stare at me like I've suggested stringing him in a tree.

"I thought you'd want to help," Yasmine says. "I thought you liked the baldies."

"I love them." Sky's howl of pain for his relative is my howl.

"Burying is bad," Gomez says. "Even for a baldie."

"Especially for a baldie," Yasmine says.

"That's ridiculous," I say.

Yasmine shrugs like she doesn't care if a dingbatter believes her or not.

"What about all the baldies that die in the woods? Do you go looking for them to make sure their devil spirits are burned?"

"If it dies in the woods, it's okay," Yasmine explains. "That's its home, and we stay out of there. But this baldie doesn't belong here." She grabs one of the dog's legs, and Gomez grabs his head. They pull the animal toward the ocean, united in blood and beliefs.

With Sky's spirit howling beside me, I wonder if there's something to what Yasmine said. I buried Sky instead of burning him. I don't think he's a devil spirit, but his spirit is here, instead of wherever spirits usually go. Is he really my gift, or is he here for some other reason?

"Okay, I'll help." I run over to them and take the part of the animal that's dragging in the sand. I study the dog for signs of how he died, but he doesn't have any visible wounds. Like he was lured to sea and drowned. Were you lured, too, Sky?

Sky stops howling and follows us to the water, sniffing the sand as if for clues. It's not unusual to find dead animals on the beach—crabs, jellyfish, the occasional dolphin—especially after a storm. But a baldie? Yasmine's right. He doesn't belong here.

"What if you found a dead fish? Do you have to burn it?" I ask.

Gomez cracks up and rolls his eyes at Yasmine. "Now who's being ridiculous?"

I'm not sure what's so funny, or if that's a yes or a no. Maybe a no since I've never seen anyone on the beach burning fish. I guess the ocean is where fish live, so it's okay?

"I'll go get a lighter and a pallet." Gomez runs off. The sun has finished setting, and it's dark. I watch him leave. The only part of him I can still see is his white T-shirt racing over the dunes.

Yasmine and I wait with the dead baldie. "It's so wet it'll be hard to light. We can use driftwood for kindling. We'll have to be careful not to burn ourselves."

I nod.

"Had to do this for my pet turtle last year."

"You had a pet turtle?" Except for the Selnicks, who keep a horse, I don't know anyone else on the island with a pet.

Yasmine nods. "Mom says they don't live as long in captivity. She should have told me that *before* he died."

"I'm sorry."

Gomez comes back with a lighter, and Nector is with him, carrying a wooden pallet.

"Hey," Nector says.

"Hey." I can't think what else to say, so I watch Sky. He paces around the dead baldie like it makes him anxious. The wet-dog smell crashes into my nose like a storm wave. Overhead, an eagle circles. I'm not sure how, but I know it's my eagle, the one I freed from Mrs. Borse's house. How could I *know*?

But I do.

She's not here to feed. I smell her sorrow. Like a rotten holly bush. An eerie feeling swims inside me. "When was the last storm?" I ask.

"Tuesday, May 6, high winds, tropical storm," Nector replies.

You can count on the Hatterasks to know about storms. It's already June. The storm was over five weeks ago.

"Why do you want to know?" Yasmine asks.

"I'm wondering how this baldie died." And how Sky died. And the baldie in Mr. Selnick's yard. This makes the third dead baldie.

"Who cares?" Gomez says, kicking off his shoes and tossing them up the beach.

"I care." I'm outnumbered three to one, but I'm sick of people not caring. I look at Yasmine. "What if he was your pet turtle? What if no one cared that he died?"

The three of them stare at me as if waiting for the punch line. Finally Nector says, "But he's not a turtle."

"Or a pet," Yasmine says.

"I know that!" My voice rises to match my anger. "He's a dog. A dog who hasn't done anything to you. Why should it matter he's not a turtle? He's dead, and that's what matters. That's what's bad. Not if we bury him or burn him."

"He's a baldie," Yasmine says.

"See, I told you she wanted to bury him," Gomez says to Nector. He makes a motion around his ear with his finger, meaning I'm crazy.

It dawns on me that Gomez made Nector come along to make sure I didn't stop them from burning the baldie. I'm so furious I can't decide if I want to keep helping them.

I wanted to bury Sky because I wanted a place to visit him. I wasn't ready to let him go. I wanted him to be part of the island where I live. Always. And I'm sad about Sky's relative, I really am, and I want to understand what killed him, but I don't need to visit him.

I force myself to speak calmly. "If you want to burn the baldie, it's fine with me. That wasn't my point." I want to shake them. Make them see this animal is not the devil. A baldie is as worthy as a turtle. But I won't convince them. No matter what I say.

So I help them load the baldie on the pallet in silence. Sky watches from the shore. The wind is strong, and it's hard to get the fire going. But we light the kindling first, and finally the pallet catches. We push him out to sea.

When I get home, I hate it that Sky can't come inside with me. He paces at the bottom of the steps. I wait with him awhile. I think about sleeping in the yard. I wish I could put my head in his soft fur. But I can't. So I tuck the dog tag in my pocket and watch him disappear.

GRAVE TRICKS

AFTER SCHOOL ON MONDAY, DAD'S STILL sleeping, so I force him to wake up. "You have to eat." I move a spoonful of soup to his lips. It took me an hour to find the can of chicken noodle in the mess of boxes.

Dad sips the spoonful, then turns his head into the pillows.

"You have to eat more," I insist.

He groans but takes another sip.

"I don't want you to get dehydrated. I better get Dr. Wade." I stand up.

Dad shakes his head and moans no.

"Are you *sure* you're sick because of the gift?"

Dad nods.

It doesn't make sense. "What about Mr. Selnick? Why is he sick? What does he have to do with us?"

"It's my fault. I scared him."

"Being scared can't make you sick," I argue.

"Being scared is the worst sickness." Dad coughs like talking hurts him. "We must use our gift to provide courage. It's the Holden way."

I don't understand, but Dad looks tired. And I have a more pressing question. "Can you see ghosts with the gift? Did you ever see Mom?"

"Spirit," Dad warns.

"Dad, I'm trying to understand. I want to help us."

"I know you do, and you will. You'll help us all."

"How? How will I help?"

"I had a dream, and the Greats told me you would." Dad has a coughing fit.

I get excited. "The Greats? They contacted you, too?"

But Dad is still coughing. He shakes his head, letting me know he can't talk anymore. I tuck him into the blankets, and in seconds his eyes flutter closed and his breathing gets deep. I place a glass of water and the bowl of soup by his bed, and quietly step outside. I want to ask him what he dreamed and if he had a vision. I want to know more about the Greats and the message they sent. But until Dad gets better, I think I have to find my own answers.

THE MINUTE I'M OFF THE FRONT PORCH, I touch Sky's dog tag. He appears, and all my fears wash away. He's got his pheasant in his mouth. So I toss it, and he leaps into the air. The joy seems to burst off him like a firecracker. I'm so happy I could burst, too. When it's me and Sky together, I can't worry.

He dashes back to me with the pheasant like he can't wait to get to me. I love that about Sky. Every time we're apart, even if it's just for the length of a pheasant throw, he acts like we've been separated for years. Maybe to him we have. Time seems to do something impossible when I'm with him. When I got home from the beach last night, it was so late I couldn't believe it. Dad would've been upset if he'd been awake to realize.

I could keep throwing the pheasant all afternoon, but Sky stops and gives me his *Follow me* stare. So I follow. And follow some more. We walk the whole island until we get to the dune where he is buried. He stands on top of his grave, staring at the ocean. The wind blows back his ears, making him look like a flag on a hill. Instead of a grave marker, I got Sky himself. Or his ghost anyway.

The pheasant I placed here is gone. I assume

it's in my hand now—that Sky's ghost picked it up on the way out of his grave.

Whooping wowzers!

Suddenly, I know how to turn the kibble into magic.

I run off the dune, but Sky doesn't want to follow. He stands on his grave still and strong, ears back, chest up, his legs straight and unmoving. *Stay,* he commands with his stance.

"Come, boy. I have a surprise."

He doesn't budge.

"We'll be right back to this spot in a minute. I promise."

Sky continues to stand on his grave, asking me to stay.

"Are you trying to tell me your grave is special?"

Sky doesn't answer. He doesn't move from his spot.

"I get it, buddy, but we have to go home for the kibble. Let's go!"

Yet Sky still doesn't want to come.

So I leave him. I stop every now and then and

look back, like he does for me. I do this until finally he follows.

AT HOME I RACE TO RETRIEVE THE DOG FOOD. I leap off my front porch toward Sky, excited to try my experiment. But I have to scramble back, because Nector skids on his bike nearly running over us. "Watch it!" I yell. I'm guessing his bike would go right through Sky, but last time I checked I wasn't invisible.

"Sorry," he says. "I was going so fast . . . and the sand is slick." He stands over his bike like he might ride away with his tail between his legs.

I remember my offer for supplies. "Do you need something?"

"What kind of cereal do you have?"

I set down the bag of kibble. Telling my invisible baldie to *stay* would probably freak Nector out, so I tuck the dog tag in my pocket and Sky disappears.

"We order one box a week, and it was Yasmine's turn to pick. Hers is too sweet for me. Not to mention that it's pink." Nector makes a face. "It's enough to make me not want to wake up tomorrow morning."

"I'm sure we have a few choices."

He smiles and gets off his bike.

"Come on in."

He hesitates at the door like he isn't sure he should step inside a dingbatter's house. Of course Nector has never been inside my house, because his mother thinks we bite. Or she thought Sky would. I wonder what Nector would say if he knew seconds ago Sky was standing beside him. Would he run away screaming about devil spirits?

"Go on." I give him a little push. "We don't make deliveries."

"Ha-ha." He steps inside. "Wowzers. It looks like you just moved in."

"Yeah." Lucky for Nector, I happen to remember seeing cereal while I was looking for soup, so I take him to the green room.

"You keep cereal in the bedroom?"

"Don't you?"

Nector shakes his head. He doesn't get the joke.

"I'm kidding. I know it's weird. We have more food than will fit in the kitchen."

"It's crazy how much stuff you have." Nector steps around the open boxes. "If you saw it, you'd think our house was empty."

"I did see. I was in your house once." I decide to ask about his loose floorboards even though I'm scared of the answer. "Why does your floor open like a trapdoor?"

"Helps the house handle a hurricane. The water rushing in has to go somewhere. Mom makes us keep blow-up rafts by all the beds, too. So we can float out." He shrugs. "When it comes to the weather, we know our future."

"Why do you think hurricanes chase your family?" I dig through some boxes and pull out three different kinds of cereal.

"Because I'm such a fast swimmer?"

I'm a fast swimmer, too, and hurricanes don't chase me. I almost say so, but Nector cracks a smile.

"Ha-ha," I say. Who knows why, right? Maybe instead of a gift, the Hatterasks got a curse. Our gift feels like a curse at the moment, with Dad too sick to get out of bed.

Nector studies the cereal boxes.

"I'm sorry. I guess we only have three choices," I say. "Cereal goes bad after a while. Dad has a tendency to order more of the nonperishables like canned goods."

"Can I have this one?" He holds up a box that comes with a free airplane toy.

"Sure."

He pulls out some dollar bills. "How much do I owe you?"

"No, silly. You can have it. We're not the general store."

"Are you sure I can't give you something for it?"

"Will you let me do a reading for you? I need to practice, and I don't have anyone to practice on."

"I heard about how your dad lost his sight."

"How did you hear that?"

Nector shrugs. "It's a small island."

"Yeah."

He passes over his house key.

As soon as I touch it, I get a jolt of nausea, so I take it to Dad's special card table and lay it down, because I don't want to throw up. But I realize if I don't hold it, I can't *see* anything.

"Don't tell my mom, okay?" Nector asks.

"I wouldn't. I can keep a secret."

We sit down, and Nector looks as nervous as I feel. His eyes follow the fan in the corner like he's not sure what to look at.

"What would you like Spirit to ask the spirits?" I sound so hokey I crack up. I have no idea how Dad starts a reading.

Nector leans forward like he can't wait to find out. "Will I get to be a pilot?"

"Okay." I pick up his key. It's warm. I take a deep breath. I concentrate on his question, and after a few seconds the nausea passes. A good start.

I close my eyes, and all is dark. I don't *see*

anything, but I *know* I'm in Nector's home by the smell. His house smells like yaupon tea and fresh wood. My imagination fills in the blanks. The white walls, the removable floors, the rafts by the beds. I feel the pull of his family, his house, the island. The house is solid even in its impermanence. A place to start, a place to return.

When I get comfortable, I feel the rumble of a big engine. I smell smoke. I think it's from the engine. The sensation of tilting. It's cold, and I shiver. My stomach flops like a fish on the dock. I've never been on a plane before, but this nauseating exhilaration must be what it feels like. The key begins to vibrate in my hand, matching the engine's rumble.

"Stop!" Nector puts his hand over mine.

I place the key on the table. It lies still.

He looks scared. He takes his key and buries it back in his shorts pocket.

"What's wrong?"

He shakes his head. "I changed my mind. I don't want to know anything."

"Are you sure?" I smile to let him know it's okay. "I think you might like the answer."

His face brightens. "Really?"

"But if you don't want to know . . . ," I tease.

"Okay. Yes."

"Yes, what?"

His head bobs vigorously. "Yes, I want to know."

"The key says you will fly," I pronounce.

"What? Really?"

"Really."

"What did you see?"

"Nothing. But I felt it."

He jumps up from the table whooping wowzers and pumping his hand in the air.

I laugh. I'm happy the gift decided to show me something. Maybe Dad's right and everything is going to be okay.

Nector grabs the cereal. "Come on."

"Where?"

"Bike ride. If you ride fast enough, it can feel like flying."

We go outside, and I see the bag of kibble. I tie

it in my bike basket with a small bungee cord. Nector puts his cereal in his backpack. I'm glad he doesn't ask me about the kibble. I want to swing by Sky's grave if I have the chance. I promised Sky we'd be right back, and I don't want it to be a lie.

Nector and I hop on our bikes and ride. I clutch Sky's dog tag so he can run beside us. He leaps and bounds, and we all hoot with joy. Nector's right. If you ride fast enough, it feels like flying.

When we get near his grave, Sky darts away from me like he's a magnet and the grave is a refrigerator. He stands on top of his dune, still and tall like a statue.

I want to put the kibble on Sky's grave, because I'm pretty sure this will turn the kibble into magic. But I can't think how to explain it to Nector without telling him my baldie is buried in that spot. Sky watches me with his intense eyes. He's trying to tell me something standing like that, but I don't know what. *Are you hungry, boy?*

Nector has his eyes in the sky looking for planes. It's my chance. I grab the kibble and drop it on Sky's grave.

"I don't see any," Nector says. He sounds disappointed.

"Yeah. Me either." Planes don't fly over this island very often. The nearest airport is on the mainland, and planes usually take a different route.

We walk on the beach for a minute staring into the clouds, and I wonder how I can feed Sky without Nector seeing.

"Oh no," Nector says.

"What?"

We're so busy looking up, Nector's foot has crushed an oyster. He pokes at the shell, and his face falls. "Shoot, I killed it." He takes it to the ocean and rinses it off, then offers it to me. "Do you want to eat it or should I?"

"I'm not hungry."

"Me either," he says. But he closes his eyes and whispers, "Thank you," to the creature in the shell. Then he pops it in his mouth.

"Why did you have to eat it?"

"You know. I took its spirit," he says.

But I don't know. Six years and I still don't

know everything islanders believe. Dad says that this island has more superstitions than you can shake a stick at and that we'll never learn them all.

"It's wrong to take a soul. The only way to make it right is to eat it. Then it's not wasted."

"Oysters have souls?" I'm surprised I never thought about it before.

"Of course. Everything has a spirit," Nector says.

"But you eat them," I argue, even though I love the idea that an oyster has a spirit.

"I had to. Don't you like oysters?"

"I do. I guess I thought if it had a soul you shouldn't eat it."

"Then you would starve. Everything has a spirit."

"Shrimp?"

Nector nods.

"Clams?"

Nector nods.

"Bananas?"

Nector nods.

"How does a banana have a spirit?"

Nector shrugs. "It's alive, isn't it?"

"I guess so, or it used to be . . . maybe. The tree it came from is."

"See?"

"What about baldies?"

Nector shakes his head. "Not the same."

"What do you mean *not the same*? They're alive. More alive than a banana."

"Yes, but they have the devil spirit. You shouldn't eat the devil spirit."

"Of course I'm not going to eat a dog." I throw up my hands and stomp back toward our bikes.

"What's wrong?" Nector chases after me. "I wouldn't eat a baldie either. I agree with you."

"No. We definitely do not agree." I hop on my bike, snatch up the kibble from Sky's grave, and take off.

"Where are you going?" Nector calls after me.

But I'm riding away so fast I'm flying.

MRS. FISHBORNE'S FUTURE

I PLAY WITH SKY THE WHOLE RIDE HOME from the beach. My anger at Nector cools so fast it's like I drank yaupon tea before I even knew I'd get mad. Sky is better than any tea. I toss the pheasant, and when he brings it back I reward him with some kibble. He gobbles up the food like he hasn't eaten in weeks. And I guess he hasn't. He chases after my bike with renewed energy and exuberance. I'm so excited. Dropping the bag of food on Sky's grave turned the kibble into something he can eat. Something that exists in my world and his. *It works, boy! I figured something out.*

Sky wags his tail in approval, but after a minute his eyes dart around like there's something worrying him that I *haven't* figured out. "What is it?"

He runs ahead, and I follow until we get to the Selnicks' house. A crowd of neighbors, including Dad, are gathered outside. Sky doesn't want to stop, but I do.

"What's going on? Is everything all right?"

Dad nods.

I'm happy to see him out of bed, but he looks pale.

"I stopped by to check on Mr. Selnick." He frowns at all the people. "I'm not the only one concerned."

"We're trying to find out what's wrong with him," Mr. Fishborne chimes in, glaring at Dr. Wade.

"I wish I could give a better diagnosis." The doctor scratches his head.

"I heard it's something caused by those devil baldies," someone—I can't see who—calls out.

There's a murmur of agreement from the crowd.

"My wife found a dead baldie in our oyster stand yesterday," Mr. Fishborne adds. "Never heard of baldies turning up dead all over town like this. Something's got to be done."

Another dead baldie? The creepy, sweaty feeling sweeps over me, but there's no freezer nearby to cure it.

"Now don't panic, but"—Dr. Wade holds up his hands in front of the Selnicks' door like he's trying to push everyone back—"this thing might be contagious, so you all shouldn't come inside the house. The man needs his rest."

"I brought his favorite casserole." Mrs. Dialfield holds up a large covered dish with two potholdered hands. "Surely it'll be okay to say hello and drop it off."

"Leave anything you want to give the Selnicks outside," Dr. Wade says. "And stay in your homes away from other people."

"I've got to teach school tomorrow," Mrs. Dialfield points out. Her face looks the way it does when a student gives an answer she doesn't like.

"We can't be expected to stop our lives," Eder complains. "I've got businesses to run. Things to do. People just need to stay away from those—"

Dad grabs my arm and lurches over into the Selnicks' bushes. I rub Dad's back as he pukes. Eder looks horrified.

The crowd backs up. There're more mutterings, and Tomasena Fishborne, who's fourteen and the oldest, bossiest girl on the island, points at Dad and screams, "He's got the devil's sickness, too!"

"He does not," I yell back at her. "You don't know what you're talking about."

"Go home, everyone! I mean it," Dr. Wade hollers. "I can't take care of all of you at the same time. Last thing we need is for this to turn into another plague."

There's a sharp intake of breath. Then the

crowd scatters quickly, with people pushing and shoving like they can't wait to get away now. Dad gives a disappointed sigh, but he doesn't seem to have the energy to tell everyone how ridiculous they're being. He leans on my shoulders, and I help him back to our house.

AFTER DAD'S SETTLED BACK IN BED, I ASK HIM why Dr. Wade was talking about a plague.

"I imagine he's referring to the old baldie legend."

"Mrs. Borse told me one," I say. "There was smallpox in it."

"There are lots of stories about the baldies, but I think Dr. Wade is referring to the one that started it all."

"There's one that started it all?" I get excited, because maybe it can help me understand. "Tell me!"

Dad takes a ragged breath. "Okay, and then

you have to let me sleep. I'm sorry, but being out and about has tired me."

I wish I had more than a few minutes with Dad awake. But I see how his eyes are ringed in dark circles and his cheeks don't have their usual flush. "I promise I'll be extra quiet for the rest of the day so you can sleep."

"Thank you. Now I'll tell myself a bedtime story, and you can listen." Dad gives me a wink. "The story goes back to when this island was first settled. A terrible sickness occurred. It caused fever, night terrors, boils, you name it. People lost their teeth and their hair, and more than half the folks who lived here died." Dad pauses. "Back then, people having dogs as pets was commonplace."

"Then why does everyone hate them now?"

"Because the first sign of sickness on the island started with a young boy's dog. The dog was feverish and stumbling around, and the family wanted to put the poor creature out of its misery. But their son wouldn't let go, no matter how much they tried to reason with him. The boy hung on to his dog day and night, crying, until all of a sudden the dog was healed but the boy died. People thought something strange was going on—like maybe the dogs had something devilish in them that let them pass the sickness on."

"What? That's crazy," I say.

Dad puts his hand on mine. "Sometimes other people's beliefs seem crazy, but it's important for us to try to understand. Remember what happened on the mainland when people didn't understand my gift?"

I nod. Dad was accused of practicing witchcraft and of being a thief and a fake. Usually by people who didn't even pay for a reading.

"People need reasons for tragedy. When this happened all those years ago, the dogs thrived, while all their owners died. The dogs claimed the island for themselves. And for a decade it was theirs. They ruled this place. Every time new settlers tried to come, the baldies chased them off. People thought it was the devil living inside the dogs that made them vicious and wild. The Hatterasks were the only family for a long time brave enough to live among them."

"The Hatterasks?"

"Not even the largest beast on the planet can take down a Hatterask." Dad smiles.

I smile, too, because I know the Hatterasks used to be whalers before too many fishermen came and the whales were all killed. In school we learned that whalers were big money and fishermen would follow them down the coast. Bald Island was such a good spot for whaling that sometimes whalers would settle here with their families. This must be how the island got repopulated.

"But wait," I say after a minute. "I still don't understand. Why does Dr. Wade think two sick people and a bunch of dead baldies will turn into a plague?"

Dad shrugs like he doesn't understand it either. His eyes get heavy, and I think he's going to fall asleep before he can answer. But after a minute he seems to come to a conclusion. "I think Dr. Wade is worried history will repeat itself."

THE NEXT MORNING, DR. WADE STANDS beside the schoolhouse doors yelling as we walk in, "Children with a fever or stomachache should notify Mrs. Dialfield immediately. She will contact me so that you can receive proper care." He repeats this over and over as we file into the classroom.

Nector and I share a look. No one wants to be sick today.

The schoolhouse doesn't have air-conditioning, only fans, and as the day goes on, things heat up. It's hard not to feel sick.

Mrs. Dialfield circles the room asking everyone what he or she wants to accomplish in the future. She says the last week of the school year is a good time to set goals for our lives.

Nector says he wants to fly an airplane.

Yasmine and Gomez say they want to win the world record for paddleball.

Behind me, the Fishborne kids talk about the dead baldie their mother found in their oyster stand at the fish market. Mrs. Fishborne moved it to the beach herself to burn. Now she isn't feeling well.

Tomasena taps me on the shoulder. "Can you help us?" She presses her house key into my hand. "Nector told us you can see the future."

I look at her in surprise.

"My mother might be sick, too," she whispers.

Mrs. Dialfield eyes them. "Are you talking about your future goals, Tomasena? I want you to think hard about what you want to accomplish."

The littlest Fishborne raises his hand.

"Yes, Kelvin," Mrs. Dialfield says.

"We don't have to think about our future. Spirit can tell us. We want to find out about our mom. Please," Kelvin begs, "I'm afraid she might die."

Mrs. Dialfield's eyes widen at the word *die.* She

notices the key in my hand. "Are you able to know things like that, Spirit?"

"I think so. I can try."

"Has your father taught you to"—Mrs. Dialfield pauses as if searching for how to put it—"pepper your readings with hope?"

I think of how Dad said it's our job to help people find the courage to face what lies ahead. "Yes."

"Five minutes at the end of our lesson, okay?"

The class cheers.

After that Mrs. Dialfield does her best to make us work on our essays, but everyone's focused on the clock. When it's time, all the kids pull their desks closer and lean in, curious and excited to see me do a reading. When Sky was around, everyone acted like I was covered in fleas or something. Baldie fleas. Now I'm so hot under their gaze I can barely think. Is it the key or the heat making me nauseous? Get it together. Don't throw up.

I grip the Fishbornes' key in my hand and try to receive what it has to tell me. Everything is pitch black. As usual. I can't *see* anything. But I'm in their house. Or I think so because it smells like seawater and vegetables—oyster stew. I smell smoke like the stew is burning. Smoke so thick it makes me cough. The smoke smells like it did when I read for Nector. But I don't think I'm on a plane. I'm still in the Fishbornes' house. There's heat so hot it's burning my skin. Like a fire. I feel fire. There's going to be another fire!

We have to get out of the house, a voice says. It sounds like Tomasena.

Where's Daddy? Kelvin's voice. He's crying. *I'm scared.*

Me too, Tomasena says. *Take my hand and close your eyes. We're going to jump like acrobats in the circus.*

My eyes snap open, because I think they're about to jump out a window.

"What happened? Did it work?" Tomasena asks.

I nod, unsure how to tell her that her house is going to catch on fire—never mind how to phrase it hopefully.

"Is our mother okay?" Kelvin asks.

"That isn't what the key showed me."

"Well, what did you see?" Tomasena leans forward, and the rest of the class leans in, too.

I'm so hot I can't breathe.

Mrs. Dialfield takes note of me. "Are you okay?" Her voice rises. "Are you sick?"

I shake my head. Can't be sick. Don't be sick.

"Your face is red and you're sweating. And you look like you have the chills," Mrs. Dialfield says.

"She was shaking when she held the key," Kelvin points out.

Was I? Dad shakes when he gives readings, too.

Our teacher feels the top of my head like she's checking for a fever.

"Readings give Holdens the shakes," I explain.

"If you feel sick, let me know, okay?" Mrs. Dialfield says.

"I'm not going to be sick." But I can barely see through the sweat. The straight blue lines on my notebook paper turn into waves. Nector's reading didn't make me feel this awful. Maybe I'm not supposed to give readings so close together when I'm starting out.

Mrs. Dialfield doesn't look convinced, and the Fishbornes move their desks back an inch. My other classmates follow. They hug the walls like Sky is with me again, and they're afraid.

I'm afraid, too. Afraid of being the messenger. How does Dad do it? Once when I complained that I hadn't inherited the gift, he said, *The gift isn't always cake on your birthday.* He was right. Even though it isn't easy, it's my job to tell the Fishbornes what their key told me.

I take a deep breath and push back the sick. Dad didn't describe every detail of his vision with Mr. Selnick. He focused on what Mr. Selnick needed to do in order to be safe. "Prepare for a fire," I tell them. "Stay on the first floor of your house so you can escape easily. Keep the windows open. Oh, and . . ." I remember Kelvin's concern for their father. "Keep track of your dad."

Tomasena's eyes widen.

"Don't be scared. You'll prepare, and you'll be ready." I try to sound braver than I feel.

"When is it going to happen?" Kelvin asks. I feel terrible. He's only seven, and he looks like he's going to cry.

"Your dad knew which tree was going to fall on our house and on what day," Tomasena complains.

"I wish I could help more, but this is all I *know*."

"So we have to stay on the first floor forever?" Kelvin asks. "But my bedroom is upstairs and all my toys—"

"That's enough," Mrs. Dialfield says. "Spirit's told you what she knows. Now let her be."

The heat is unbearable, and the reading has made me feel drained and exhausted. I try not to slide off my seat into a puddle of sweat. But it isn't easy. To distract myself, I hold Sky's tag. He appears outside the school window, tail wagging.

I wish we could run off together into the woods under some cool, shady trees. Instead I'm so hot, I see double. I wipe my eyes. It doesn't help. There's still more than one Sky. More than two.

He's brought three friends?

I release Sky's tag. But only Sky disappears.

His friends stay. They look too young to be dead. They're ghost puppies like Sky.

I count the dead baldies of Bald Island. The one from Mr. Selnick's yard, the one Yasmine and Gomez found on the beach, and now the one at the fish market. Then of course there's Sky.

Four dead baldies.

Four ghost puppy baldies.

They bark at me. A chorus of howls. I touch Sky's tag again, and he joins them. The barking is so loud it sounds like there are dogs inside my eardrums instead of outside the window. I put my hands over my ears, but it doesn't help. The bell rings, and kids shuffle around me, gathering their things. The classroom empties, but I don't move. The Fishbornes don't leave either. They stop to stare. The noise rises with the heat, and the sick goes high tide in my throat. I lurch forward, and I hear the Fishbornes scream.

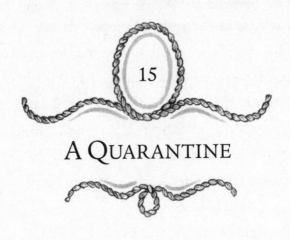

15

A QUARANTINE

"I'M SORRY," I SAY. MY STOMACH SWIRLS AND
spins. I try to sit as still as I can to settle it.

Mrs. Dialfield calms us with her steady voice.
"There's cleaner under the sink. Can you get it for
me, Tomasena? Kelvin, can you get us some paper
towels?"

The Fishbornes hand Mrs. Dialfield what she
needs. Then they back *waaaay* up from the sick I
made on the floor. Mrs. Dialfield dives in, clean-
ing without their help.

"We better have the doctor look at you," she says to me when she's finished.

"But the reading is what made me sick."

"The reading made you sick?" Mrs. Dialfield looks surprised.

I nod. "Because I'm still learning."

"Huh," she says like she's still worried.

"It's okay. It'll go away once I have the courage to face my today."

Mrs. Dialfield's face relaxes. "That's very wise."

"Please don't send for the doctor. No one can know. Puking is bad for business."

Mrs. Dialfield laughs. "Okay. Your secret is safe with me. What do you think, Tomasena? Kelvin? Can you keep Spirit's secret?"

"You won't tell, will you?" I plead.

Tomasena watches me as if she's trying to decide if helping a dingbatter is allowed. After a few seconds she nods.

But little Kelvin shakes his head. "I'm not good at keeping secrets."

"Can you try?" Mrs. Dialfield asks.

"Okay," Kelvin says after a moment. "I can't promise though, because it might be a lie."

"Fair enough," Mrs. Dialfield says.

We gather our things, and as soon as I'm outside in the fresh air I feel good enough to hop on my bike and fly home.

But halfway there, I stop riding and rub Sky's tag. I wonder if all the wild ghost baldies will appear again. They disappeared when I threw up. But it's just Sky, wagging his tail, wanting to play Fetch the Pheasant. He sticks his rear end in the air and grins.

I frown. "Something horrible is going on, buddy. Baldies dead all over town. Fires in our futures. Can you tell me what's happening? Why did you die? Were you sick? Were your friends sick? Why are *people* sick?"

I walk beside my bike so he and I can talk.

"You were the first one, boy. The first that I know of. It started with you. Do you *know* things? You must. You're here to tell me, aren't you?"

But Sky only picks up the pheasant and drops it at my feet. I sigh and toss it for him.

The pheasant sails through the air. Sky leaps toward it and raises his nose, like he wants to make sure I'm watching his big blue namesake. He's right, something's up. Real birds appear. They form a V shape, an arrow that points to an eagle. My eagle, the one from Mrs. Borse's house! She's carrying something in her mouth. She drops it, and it falls from the heavens and knocks the pheasant out of the air. I run over to see what it is.

It's a thick, heavy rope with a note pinned to it. Sky sniffs the rope while I unpin the piece of paper.

A great rope for a great moment
A great hope you'll know when
To unlock the magic
Of this great rope
Granted you by the Greats

Another gift from the Holden Spirits! "Look, boy. A rope!" I pick up the eagle's gift.

But Sky is already bored with it.

"Huh. You're right, buddy. Looks like any old rope to me, too."

Sky walks away like, even though he wanted me to find it, he doesn't know what it's for either.

A great hope you'll know when

Well, all righty, then. I stuff the rope in my backpack for later. "Thanks!" I yell to the eagle. She dips down as if to say *You're welcome*, then flies away.

Sky wags his tail, drops the pheasant at my feet, and then grins up at me for a treat.

"You think you should be rewarded for helping me find this rope, huh? I suppose that's fair." I pull the bag of kibble from my backpack and feed him a piece.

We ride toward home playing Fetch the Pheasant until Sky suddenly stops. He won't bring the pheasant back.

"Come on, boy. Bring it here for your treat," I call.

But he won't come. He barks and circles under something posted on a tree. Sky's ability to spot something new or different about his surroundings is amazing. There's a sign on the tree that reads:

BEWARE OF BALDIES
Baldies have transmitted an unknown
sickness to our beloved island.
Those contaminated have been quarantined.
Anyone with symptoms of illness
should contact Dr. Wade.

I don't need a key to tell me this means bad news for the future. I drop my bike in the road and grab my walkie-talkie to call Dad.

"Zookeeper calling Big Panda." My radio spits static in response. I try again. "Come in, Big Panda." More static.

I keep trying to call Dad on the radio, but he doesn't answer. He always answers.

"Zookeeper? Red Baron here." Nector's voice garbles through the radio instead of Dad's.

"Your dad is with Dr. Wade," Nector says. "Mr. Selnick burned that baldie. Did your dad help? Both of them are really sick. Copy that?"

"But . . ." Dad is sick because of the gift, not because of a baldie. He said so.

"Zookeeper, do you copy?"

"No, you're wrong. Dad—"

"Meet me at your house in five?"

I agree. "Over and out."

I pick up my bike and hop on. Sky runs beside me with a new urgency. Something terrible is going to happen. I feel it, and I think Sky does, too.

When I skid up to the house, the Hatterask kids are waiting for me on the front steps.

Yasmine stands. "We have to turn ourselves in."

"What? Why?"

"We touched that baldie on the beach." She rubs her hands on her pink shorts like that'll get the germs off.

I stare from her to her brothers. "So?"

"So we should tell Dr. Wade," Gomez says as if I'm stupid. He picks up his bike.

"But we're not sick," I argue.

"We should probably tell," Nector agrees. "My mom says they've taken your dad and Mr. Selnick to the old whale station."

The whale station is an abandoned carcass of a building on a nearby barrier island called Whales' Cove. It sits alone with a bunch of old oil drums and giant bones.

"They've locked them up," Nector continues. "No one's allowed in or out. They're asking anyone who touched a baldie to come forward."

"They can't do that," I say, even though I have no idea who *they* is and if *they* can or not. "My dad shouldn't be there. This isn't why he's sick."

"It reeks of seagull poop and whale guts in there," Gomez says. He moves his foot off his bike pedal and puts it back on the ground like maybe he isn't in such a hurry to be locked up in the whale station after all.

"Not to mention it's haunted," Yasmine adds.

Yasmine and Gomez share a scared look.

I squeeze the dog tag in my palm, thinking hard. Sky thumps his tail, like he's thinking, too. "I don't feel sick. And I refuse to believe baldies make people sick until I have proof." I have a terrible feeling about all this. Like I'm holding the key to all our futures and things are going to turn out bad if I don't do something. But what? I think for a minute, then I decide. "I'm not going to volunteer to be shut away in the smelly whale station, and none of you should either."

"What if we're contagious and we make other people sick?" Yasmine looks worried.

"The first sign of sickness, we'll tell someone," I say. "Until then, we have to stick together or we're all going to end up there." I look at Nector.

He nods. Gomez and Yasmine do, too.

My handle comes across our walkie-talkies. "Repair Wizard calling Zookeeper. Got your ears on?" Repair Wizard—that's Mr. Hatterask.

"Zookeeper here," I answer.

"Zookeeper, report to Repair Wizard's house tonight. Copy that?"

Yasmine steps forward. "Since your dad's sick. You're going to stay with us, okay?"

Nector nods, but Gomez looks like he's going to object. His sister elbows him in the side.

"What's going on?" I ask Mr. Hatterask over the walkie-talkie.

"Dr. Wade is taking care of your dad. He doesn't want you or anyone else to be infected. And you can't stay by yourself."

I have questions, so I start firing them off. "How does Dr. Wade know the baldies are to blame? How can it be their fault?"

"I know it must be frightening. I'm sorry," Mr. Hatterask says. "All of you kids come on home, and we'll talk about it over dinner. Repair Wizard over and out."

"Zookeeper over and out," I say.

But I can't imagine Dad would rather be recovering in the old whale station. "No matter how sick, my dad would never leave me like this. He'd want me to be with him."

The Hatterask kids watch me with nervous eyes.

"If he's sick, I should be there to help take care of him. You'd do the same for your dad, wouldn't you?" I ask them.

Nector looks toward the woods behind my house.

If I go through the woods, I can take a raft to get to the cove, because the ocean distance is shortest there. Otherwise, I'll need a bigger boat. But it's a long trek through those trees.

"You can't go," Nector insists. "Dad said we should come home now."

"I want to see my dad," I say.

"It'll be dark soon," Yasmine points out. "You could get lost."

Gomez smirks, like he's hoping for it.

"I might be a dingbatter," I snap, "but I know my way around." Besides, I won't be alone. I'll have Sky. Sky is all I need.

But Yasmine speaks before I can. "We want to help, is all." She gives Gomez a long look. They seem to silently agree on something. "We should go with you. We wouldn't even be alive if it weren't for your dad. This is our chance to repay him."

I'm stunned. They never talk about what my dad did for them. And their mom acts like it was a bad thing. "That's nice of you, but . . ." I don't need their help. Dad and I have taken care of ourselves for a long time.

Nector scolds his siblings. "You know you're not allowed in the woods. What if Dr. Wade is right and you get sick?" He shakes his head. "It was so stupid of us to touch that baldie. Of course they carry bacteria and diseases. Don't you pay attention to your science lessons?"

Yasmine and Gomez lower their eyes.

I hate to admit he has a point. A deep memory surfaces of Dad making me wear gloves around Sky when we first found him, until we knew what was wrong with him. I love the baldies, but even I know they're wild.

"We had to burn him," Yasmine says to Nector, "and you helped. We're going with Spirit. She can't go alone into the woods. Are you going to tell on us? Please don't. This is our chance to repay Mr. Holden."

Nector sighs. "Well, if you go, I have to go. Someone's got to look out for you."

"Yay!" Yasmine claps her hands like she's won pink cereal instead of a sweaty hike through bug-infested woods.

"We have to tell Mom and Dad. If I radio them, they'll say no." Nector puts his hand on his walkie-talkie for a minute like he's thinking of what to do. "Gomez, you go home and tell them, and Yasmine and I will go with Spirit. By then it'll be too late for them to stop us."

Gomez shakes his head. "No way. I'm not going to be the one left out."

"I said, you go home," Nector repeats.

Gomez folds his arms. "Make me."

Nector sighs again. "Fine. I'll go home to talk to Dad then. Mom will be furious if you little brats aren't back in time for dinner. You better hurry. It's a long way."

"First we should get supplies," Yasmine says.

I think about the mosquitoes that ate up my legs last time and the ticks I was afraid would bite me. "Okay."

We say goodbye to Nector, and I invite his siblings inside the Holden supply house. I put them to work digging through boxes while I check for a note from Dad.

"Why do you need all this?" Yasmine asks. They are as amazed as Nector at the incredible stash.

I shrug. "Never know what might happen." Surrounded by Dad's thoughtful preparation, I miss him so much. I don't only need Sky. I need Dad, too. I try my walkie-talkie again, but there's no response. "He didn't leave a note. He's not answering when I call. Something's bad wrong."

"Maybe he's too sick to talk," Yasmine suggests.

There's a knock at the door. I open it to find Eder Mint. He tips his sailor's hat at me and smiles. "Everything okay here, Lavender Spirit?"

I'm not sure where to start with all that's wrong, so I say, "Yes."

Eder frowns like that isn't the answer he was expecting. "Well, I'm concerned. With your dad away, you can't be without a guardian. It isn't safe, particularly with this sickness going around. There's a children's home on the mainland where you can stay until things settle down. We can call right now—"

"I'm staying with the Hatterasks."

"What?" Eder looks flustered. "Well, I really think . . ."

Behind me Yasmine shakes her head, like she'll be really disappointed if I don't stay with her.

"I'll be all right there," I say.

"Isn't that too many kids for your parents to look after?" Eder asks Yasmine. He pokes his head around the door and sees Gomez digging through Dad's boxes. "What are you kids—"

Yasmine steps forward. "Spirit will be fine at our house. Thanks, Eder!" She closes the door before Eder can object.

I turn to her in surprise.

"That orphanage on the mainland is almost as bad as the whale station," Yasmine explains. "Mom used to joke about sending us there when we misbehaved. Trust me, you don't want to go there."

"An orphanage? But I have a dad. And I don't care what anyone says, I'm going to see him."

Yasmine nods. "Eder's just a busybody. Ignore him." But after a moment she scrunches her forehead like something doesn't add up. "I'm surprised Eder would even suggest a thing like that. He sure wouldn't go away from his *own* parents."

"What do you mean?" I ask.

"People say his mom still tucks him in at night."

I can't help laughing.

Gomez sticks his head out of a box and shouts, "She doesn't anymore!"

Yasmine shoots him a glare. "How do *you* know?"

Her brother shrugs.

"Well, she used to," Yasmine insists. "Even after he was grown and living in his own house!"

"These backpacks are cool," Gomez says. He pulls one out of a box of a dozen. It's bright orange and made from the strongest material known to man.

"We have a few buried in the yard, too," I say.

Gomez looks shocked. "Why?"

"In case the house is destroyed. We can dig them up, and the supplies inside will be okay." Dad researched backpacks for weeks, looking for the best survival packs they make. Ones that can survive earthquakes, hurricanes, fires, you name it.

Gomez stares at me in wonder.

"I know. Dad thinks of everything."

"This could be useful." Yasmine holds up a pellet gun.

"Why?" I can't imagine what Dad was thinking when he ordered that.

"Protection," Yasmine says. She doesn't mention from what, but I can guess.

"We're not going to shoot a baldie," I protest.

Yasmine loops the gun into the strap on one of the orange survival backpacks. "Like you said, you never know what might happen."

I almost protest again, but she's right. I don't *know*. Maybe if I did, Dad wouldn't be gone.

TRESPASSING

WE SPRAY OURSELVES DOWN WITH BUG SPRAY
and fill the orange backpacks with water and
food. We bring snacks like apples and carrots and
some cute little travel-size packets of peanut butter that Yasmine and Gomez got really excited
over. We also pack flashlights, a compass, a whis-
tle, and a flare in case we lose our way. A raft that's
folded into a tiny square will blow up to carry us
from the woods' edge to the barrier island of

Whales' Cove. Dad ordered so many useful things. Did he get lucky? Or did he *know*?

I think deep down he *knew* Sky was special. He used to say, *Spirit needs Sky.*

I touch his tag. *Why are you here, boy? To protect me? To lead me to Dad?*

But Sky hasn't gained the ability to speak. He stands next to us, wagging his tail, happy to be invited along on our adventure.

I don't tell Yasmine and Gomez, but Sky is leading the way. He trots out in front, tall and proud.

I grip his dog tag in my palm as we walk. His spirit is here for a reason. He has something to do with my gift. I know that now. I believe he has things to show me. When I let him, he leads. It's my job to follow.

When we get to the woods, Sky puts his nose to the ground. He seems to catch the scent of something. Something that makes him move faster.

I run after him. The other ghost baldies appear

to help blaze the trail, but the trees still far out-number the dogs.

Yasmine and Gomez lag behind. They push and shove and giggle. It's hard keeping an eye on them and the ghost baldies. I begin to regret letting the Hatterask kids come.

"We should pick up the pace," I suggest. "You don't want to be late for dinner." Really I don't want to lose Sky and his friends.

Gomez grumbles.

"Come on!" I yell, wishing I had a way to make them hurry.

But suddenly Sky stops at a tangle of brambles. His stance is firm and strong in front of the more difficult path. *This way,* his body says. The other ghost baldies stop, too. Naturally, Yasmine and Gomez run ahead, choosing a path less dense.

"Wait." I pull back some of the brambles, wishing I'd brought the gloves Dad uses when he loads and unloads boxes. "This way's better."

"Why? We'll get all scraped up," Gomez argues.

"It's a shortcut," I lie. Of course I can't know if

Sky is taking us the shortest way, but he seems to be leading us somewhere important. For all I know Dad isn't even at the whale station. Maybe Sky knows things I don't. If he's part of my gift, I have to trust him.

"How can it be a shortcut?" Gomez asks. "There's only one way—straight through."

"I'm going this way. Follow or not," I insist. I don't have any more reasons to give. The truth—that we're following the ghost of a dead baldie, four of them in fact—won't help. They wanted to come along. I can't help it if they don't like the path Sky and his friends choose.

Yasmine and Gomez share one of their looks, which I assume means, *Fine, follow the dingbatter*, because they plow after me through the brambles.

On the other side, Gomez jumps in front of me and grins. "Beat'cha." As if who got through the brambles first were a contest.

I shrug. If he wants to make a game of it, fine by me. Maybe it will make him hurry up so we don't lose Sky and his pack of ghost baldies.

Gomez seems eager to race. "Last one there's a rotten oyster." He pinches his nose and takes off.

We all tear into the woods. Unaware he's on the tail of a baldie, Gomez catches up quickly. Yasmine isn't far behind now either. It's a relief, because the deeper we go into the woods the darker it gets, making it harder to see Sky and his team through the trees.

There should be plenty of sunlight left in the day, but the trees thicken enough to block it. The occasional beams of light cast long tree-shaped shadows that manage to make the woods seem even thicker. The only path is the one we make with our bodies. The sticks and branches resist. They grab at our bags and clothes, and snap and crunch under our feet.

Now that we're playing a game, Gomez and Yasmine get serious about being fast. They ignore the woods' efforts to yank them back. They scramble over a fallen tree like it's nothing. It takes me a few tries, and I bloody my leg getting across. They're younger than me, and their legs are shorter, yet they can run faster. It's annoying I'm not quicker, because Sky and his friends are getting farther ahead, and what if they change direction?

Gomez stops to break a huge branch blocking our way. He kicks and stomps it, but he isn't strong enough to break it. Yasmine jumps on, too, and together they bounce up and down until it snaps. "Yahoo!" they cry.

Sky is ahead of them anyway and his buddies jump higher, run harder, and dodge trees with a sixth sense for where they'll be. His friends dash ahead out of sight, like they don't have Sky's loyalty and can't be bothered to wait for me.

I force my arms and legs to pump faster. The darkness deepens. I don't want to be stuck in the middle of the woods without Sky. I bragged that I knew the way, but I don't. There's supposed to be only one way, straight through, like Gomez said, but I feel twisted up. At this point, I trust Sky to know better. I've never been in the woods without him. I hadn't realized it before, but maybe Sky has always led the way.

We can't lose him.

I'm panting and sweating, and my backpack feels like it's gained a few apples. But I don't stop. Gomez and Yasmine leap ahead as if they have an infinite amount of energy. They high-five and help each other over trees and bushes like siblings who've played together their whole lives. They aren't afraid of the darkness.

It's so dark now I want my flashlight. But it's zipped up in my backpack, and if I stop to get it, I'll lose Sky.

And then I lose him anyway. He darts into a thicket of trees and, *poof*, he's gone. I can't see him anymore. I squeeze his dog tag in my sweaty hand, but it doesn't bring him back. "Sky, wait!" I scream.

"What?" Gomez calls. He and Yasmine stop running.

"Wait for me," I say, hoping they didn't hear me say Sky's name.

"Guess we know who's a rotten oyster," Gomez says.

I keep running right past them, grinning like it's still a big game, and I've tricked them into stopping while I leap ahead.

"Hey! No fair," Gomez yells as I whip by.

"Last one there's a rotten jellyfish!" I scream, upping the ante, relief rushing over me because I see my good dog. He stands at the end of the thicket, waiting.

He barks once, then leads us into another tangle of brambles.

Gomez dives into it like it's a pile of leaves instead of ouchy sticks. He's on the other side before me and Yasmine. Ahead again, he yells, "Last one there's a rotten baldie!"

I'm irritated this is the animal he picks, but I chose to play the game, so I bite back my complaint.

When I get to the other side, Gomez puts out his arm to stop me. His voice is a whisper. "Stay back."

But I've lost sight of Sky again, so I move his arm out of my way and push forward.

Then I see what Gomez sees. A cave. And Sky trotting up to the entrance. I don't think twice about following.

"No!" Gomez yells.

"I want to see what's inside."

"Get back!" Gomez tries to grab my arm, but I shake him off and keep walking toward Sky.

"Baldies!" Yasmine cries behind us as a pack of wild dogs exit the cave. They don't notice Sky. They growl a warning deep and low, but I don't act fast enough. I've followed Sky to the entrance of a cave of live baldies. One runs at me, teeth bared.

I scramble back and fall into thick bushes. The angry baldie jumps on top of me, and I scream. The brambles stab me all over as I thrash, but I can't get free. Sky is barking and trying to help, but the wild baldie can't hear or feel Sky, so he doesn't let up. I try to push the animal against his chest, but instead my arm goes right into his mouth. A sharp pain cuts into my skin.

Bam! A noise pops and the baldie whimpers a wounded cry.

"No!" I scream.

"Run!" Yasmine screams back, the pellet gun dangling from her hand.

The hit baldie retreats, and Gomez and Yasmine take off. I'm left alone in the bushes.

I try to get up, to run, but I'm stuck. I try again, but my backpack is caught on the branches. The hit baldie and his friends have turned their attention to Yasmine and Gomez. They run forward a few feet and bark at the kids' retreating backs. They stay near their home to protect it. Soon they'll notice I'm still here—too close, a threat.

I wiggle out of my backpack. I try to pull it out of the brambles, but it won't come. The baldies turn to me.

I'm not sure how I'll fare fleeing a pack of baldies that can run so much faster than any human ever could, but hanging on to this pile of brambles while being eaten alive hardly seems like the key to survival.

So I leave my bag. And I run. My heart hammers so fast it feels like a ticking bomb that could explode me into a million pieces. I'm terrified of being chased and knocked down again. The barking of the baldies seems to get louder. Are they after me? I won't be able to fend off more than one. I scream for Yasmine and Gomez, but they're gone. I took too long getting untangled.

I twist my head back to the baldies. I stop running, and relief floods my body. They haven't followed me. Not even Sky. I can't believe it. I stare in amazement, my jaw dropping. I'm running for my life, and Sky is . . . playing?

The other ghost baldies are there, too. They nudge their live friends, knocking them and running around, trying to get noticed. *Hey guys, it's us. Back from the dead,* they seem to say, hitting into their oblivious friends. But the live baldies can't see them.

They only see me.

They stare me down, their eyes a menacing black. The baldie Yasmine hit limps back into the

cave. The others bark a warning. *Don't come back.*
Another lunges at me a few steps, in case I'm
thinking of staying.

I have to leave. I tear away.

But my good dog doesn't come with me.

THE KEY TO HOME

I DON'T KNOW WHERE I AM ANYMORE. MY
backpack of supplies, my compass and flashlight,
are stuck in a bush near the baldies' home. My
forearm has bite marks that bleed streaks down
to my hand. The bite aches, and the sight of it ter-
rifies me. Yasmine and Gomez are long gone, and
Sky isn't here to lead the way. My worst fears are
realized. I'm lost and alone in the woods. I have
nothing but a metal dog tag that no longer makes
my dog appear in front of me.

I push it back into my pocket and find I have one other item. My house key. I squeeze it and concentrate on home. I don't need the future. I need a compass. But this is all I have. I abandon the idea of going to the whale station. It's dark, and I don't know the way.

The noises in the woods seem to get louder. The sound of an owl and an unidentifiable flutter in the trees cut through the silence. As much as it seemed annoying to have Yasmine and Gomez come along, now I'd give anything to have them with me. My heart hasn't stopped hammering, and I imagine it won't anytime soon. Every noise makes me jump. I check behind me for baldies whenever I hear the woods crackle and snap. The dogs have every right to chase me down. The cave I marched up to was the baldies' home. Of course they want to protect it. Mrs. Borse accused the eagle of trespassing.

We had just trespassed, too.

Oh, Sky, why? Why did you lead us to that cave? I could have gotten killed.

For the first time since I read the *Beware of*

181

Baldies poster, I'm really scared. If the baldies do carry some disease, getting a bite from one seems like a sure way to catch it. I frantically try to wipe the blood off on my shirt.

I'm sad and confused that Sky isn't here with me now. I followed him, convinced he wanted to show me something important. But what if he just wanted to play with his friends? Maybe he doesn't know anything about where Dad's been taken.

I look down at my arm. With the streaks cleaned, it looks less frightening, at least in the dark. Harmless even—the puncture marks are barely visible. I can do this. I can get out of here.

Tree branches thwack my body as I stumble through the darkness, clutching my house key. I beg it to take me home. I don't know if it has that kind of power, but it's my only hope, until a squawk brings my attention to the sky.

The trespassing eagle.

She nods as if to say, *I'll help you find home.*

Home. I look down at the key in my hand. I

thought of home when I wanted the eagle to go out the window. I started Nector's reading by smelling his home. Dad told Mr. Selnick home is an important part of who we are. Sky's tag tells a stranger how to bring him home.

Home is the magic of a person's key.

Home. I'd give anything to be in mine with Dad and Sky.

I follow the eagle through the dark woods.

I'm filled with relief when she leads me out and onto my familiar road. "Thank you," I whisper.

She flies down toward me, then back up into the sky, her way of saying, *You're welcome.*

It isn't just the woods that are dark. The road is dark, too. I have a feeling the Hatterasks' dinner hour has come and gone. The last time I chased Sky into the woods, time sped up. How long have I been gone?

I FIND OUT THAT IT'S AFTER MIDNIGHT. THE Hatterasks aren't happy. I stand in their house, an injured and guilty dingbatter.

Yasmine and Gomez were my responsibility. I led them into danger. I'm so relieved they made it home safe that it takes the sting out of Mrs. Hatterask yelling at me.

"I don't know what your father allows, but we don't let our children go in the woods," Mrs. Hatterask says.

"What took you so long?" Yasmine asks. "We've been back hours."

"I lose time," I confess, though it sounds even crazier out loud than in my head. I expect them to think so, too.

But Mrs. Hatterask pauses a minute, then nods. "Death is a thief who will snatch the day. Look at this." She holds up my arm like it's proof of something. Me being a dingbatter? The baldies' devilish nature? All of the above?

Or is she telling me I'm going to die from this baldie bite? I'm shocked.

The Hatterask kids shrug like their mom says scary, nonsensical things all the time.

Mr. Hatterask turns to his wife. "We should tend to that wound and put her to bed."

Mrs. Hatterask calms, but I wonder if it's the eye of a hurricane. Maybe she's going to kick me out or send me off to be quarantined. I've been bitten by a baldie. But she gets me antiseptic and a bandage and wraps my arm.

After she's finished, she says, "You're staying under our roof, so you obey our rules. The woods are forbidden."

I want to go home to my own bed. My own house. My own beliefs. But when I say so, her husband shakes his head. "Your father wouldn't want you to be alone. He'd want you to stay here."

I'm suddenly too tired to disagree. They feed me dinner and tuck me into bed beside Yasmine. "Aren't you worried I'm contagious?" I ask.

"We don't believe in that foolishness," Mrs. Hatterask says. "Devil wants a person, he finds them. Locking people away or hiding won't save you. I ought to know."

"Is that why you don't move houses even though the hurricane knocks yours down every year?"

She nods. "Hatterasks tried that in the early days. Didn't do a bit of good."

Their house is so empty, it's a miracle they had an extra pillow. Mr. Hatterask even brings me a raft to put beside the bed. Yasmine has one on her side, too, so it's my own.

After her parents turn out the light, Yasmine whispers, "I'm sorry."

"What for?" I wait awhile for her to answer, but her breath gets heavy and even, the breathing of dreams. I figure she's sorry for leaving me, but she shouldn't be. She saved my life shooting that pellet gun when she did. Even if I don't approve of shooting a baldie, as far as I'm concerned her debt to Dad has been repaid.

Outside the baldies howl. They remind me of a family at the dinner table talking all at once.

They speak over each other, a crowded roar of interrupting, overlapping cries. They don't usually keep me awake, but they sound more agitated than usual. I wonder if they howl for their relative who turned up dead on the beach—or maybe the one Mr. Selnick found on his lawn.

The image of the ghost baldies knocking into their live friends replays in my mind. I sit up in the bed. Maybe what looked like playing was really Sky and the others trying to warn their buddies?

Four baldies are dead. Is it possible more will die? Is it possible to save them?

No one on this island but me would care to. And then I *know*. This is what I'm meant to do. It's up to me to save Dad and the remaining baldies. I crawl out of bed, get dressed, and tiptoe into the Hatterasks' living room. I intend to go outside to see if I can conjure Sky and the other ghost baldies, but I run into Nector.

"The bathroom's this way," he says. "I'm finished up in there."

"Oh. Thanks." I stand awkwardly in the center of his living room, the front door an aggravating five feet away. I assume if the Hatterasks don't allow their kids in the woods, they also don't allow them outside in the middle of the night. Well, nearly morning at this point.

Nector gives me an odd stare. Not that I can blame him. Maybe he notices I'm wearing my sneakers.

"Can I ask you something?" He tilts his head like he's trying to figure something out.

I nod, wondering how I'll explain why I'm dressed to go outside.

"Gomez says you walked right up to that cave like you were being called into it. Were you?"

"Sort of," I say because I can't think how else to explain why I would ignore Gomez's warning.

"You should be careful," Nector says. "A great-grandfather of ours died like that."

"Like how?"

"A devil spirit led him to his death. Made him want to go swimming in a hurricane."

For once I'm at a loss for words.

Nector walks back down the hall to his room.

"Good night," I whisper. Then when he's out of sight and the coast is clear, I pull open the front door as quietly as possible and slip out.

ROTTEN OYSTER

I HOLD SKY'S TAG. HE APPEARS, HAPPY, HIS TAIL wagging, like he's a computer that's been reset. Like he's forgotten he left me for his baldie friends. "Were you trying to warn them?" I ask, not really expecting an answer.

But he runs away, stopping after a second to make sure I'm following. As usual, he wants to take me somewhere. Maybe he remembers his friends after all, because he leads me across the island to the woods' edge. But just like he can't follow me inside buildings, I can't follow him inside the woods. The other baldie ghosts appear, too, as if Sky knew he'd need help convincing me. Now there are four ghost dogs wanting me to follow.

"I'm not allowed," I tell them. "It isn't safe."

Sky looks back and forth from me to the woods, insistent. The others give me their intense *Follow me* eyes.

I hold up my bandaged arm. "You can't save me if I accidentally stumble into the baldies' home. Turns out ghost dogs aren't very useful when it comes to protection."

The Fishbornes have left their back porch light on. It reflects off my white bandages. Staring at my arm, I get an idea. If I don't get sick from this baldie bite, it's proof the baldies don't make people sick. *I'm* Dad's ticket out of quarantine.

Sky and his friends continue to stand at the woods' edge, firm in their desire for me to follow them into the trees.

I think of Nector's warning. I know Sky wouldn't lead me to my death on purpose, but if I blindly follow him, maybe it could end up that way.

I remember what Mrs. Hatterask said: *Death is a thief who will snatch the day.* In my case, Sky is a thief who snatches the night. It's almost morning, and I haven't slept a wink. I'm exhausted.

"I'm sorry I can't follow you tonight, buddy. But I'm glad to have you back." I rub the air near the top of Sky's head. It's nice, even if neither of us can feel it. "Sleep tight. I'll see you tomorrow." I tuck his tag into my pocket, return to the Hatterasks' house, and sneak back into bed.

IT CAN'T BE MUCH PAST DAWN WHEN I WAKE UP, but the bed next to me is empty. I hear Yasmine and the other Hatterasks already up and at 'em. I didn't bring an overnight bag, but one full of clothes that belong to me has appeared next to my raft. I pull on a clean T-shirt and some shorts and join the Hatterasks in the living room. "Did you go by my house?"

Mrs. Hatterask nods. "I thought you could use some fresh clothes when you woke up."

"Thanks. That's nice." I'm glad she's forgiven me for going into the woods and taking Yasmine and Gomez with me. "Have you heard from my dad?"

Mr. Hatterask clucks his tongue. "It isn't right. A man's got a right to die in his home with his family, not be cast off the line like some old shoe."

His kids stare at the floor like they don't think I'll ever hear from my dad again.

"My dad isn't going to die," I say. I have a bandaged, bitten arm, but I feel fine.

"You'll stay with us," Mr. Hatterask says. "In the comfort of our home. We'll keep it quiet."

His wife nods.

"Can we convince them to release my dad? He isn't sick because of the baldies."

Mr. Hatterask shakes his head. "I've tried, and I'll keep trying, but with everyone so frantic . . ."

"Maybe it's best he's not here for now. We can

talk more about it tonight," Mrs. Hatterask says. "You kids run by the fish market and get some oysters for me before school. Spirit, if anyone asks about your arm, you should be ready with a story that doesn't involve the baldies. If people find out, they'll lock you up, too."

"Lock me up?" That familiar sweaty feeling comes over me, like if I don't do something, everything will turn out wrong.

"You kids get moving now, run that errand for me before school so I can have something to make for dinner," Mrs. Hatterask says, shooing us out the door.

"I'll wear long sleeves." I run back to my bag and pull out the only long-sleeved clothing I can find, a sweater. It'll be sweltering, but if I lie about my arm, people won't believe me later when I say I was bitten and didn't get sick.

I'm willing to sweat for my cause.

Yasmine and Gomez play paddleball on the way to the fish market. The pink ball makes a rhythmic thwack against the wooden paddles.

Yasmine walks backward, and Nector spots her. "Tree to the left," Nector warns.

Yasmine moves right without turning her head from the ball Gomez sends her.

They're really good. I hold Sky's tag, so he runs with us. His ghost body leaps and twists, trying to catch the ball. But his mouth zooms right through the pink rubber. I don't know where the other ghost dogs are. I haven't figured out what makes them appear or disappear. Maybe Sky decides.

"They can go on for hours," Nector says. "Their record is five and a quarter."

"Wowzers." I have to walk fast to keep up. I'm already starting to see why a sweater is called a sweater. Someone obviously wore one on a hot day.

"We're going to break the world record," Yasmine says.

To distract myself from the heat, I count the number of *Beware of Baldies* posters we pass along the way. There are fifteen outside the general store, five on the doors to the schoolhouse, two at Mrs. Dialfield's, and three more at Dr. Wade's. I'm surprised Mrs. Dialfield would agree to let them be posted at her house. Has everyone been convinced the baldies are to blame?

I try Dad a few more times on the walkie-talkie, but I don't get any answer. "I want to talk to my dad."

Nector nods.

I keep counting posters. By the time we get to the fish market, I'm up to thirty-three.

Tomasena greets us at the Fishbornes' oyster stand. "What can I get you?" She and Kelvin wear stained white aprons and frazzled expressions.

"A pound, please." Nector pulls out some cash.

Tomasena digs up a scoopful of oysters and dumps them on the scale. Kelvin opens the cashbox and holds out his hand for the money.

Nector hesitates. "Where's Mr. Fishborne?" Mr. Fishborne doesn't usually let his kids touch the money or work the stand on a school day.

"Not here at the moment," Tomasena says with a false cheerfulness in her voice.

"Dr. Wade came last night to take away our

mom, and now Dad isn't feeling well," Kelvin whispers.

"Shhhh!" Tomasena whacks him on the arm with the oyster scooper.

Are they going to lock up everyone? The sweat drips down my back, and I'm sure my T-shirt underneath is soaked. I want to take off my sweater. But unless I want to be quarantined, the Hatterasks are right. I would have to lie about how I hurt my arm.

"Will you tell Mrs. Dialfield we have to work, and we won't make it to class today?" Tomasena asks.

"I'll tell her," I say.

Hovered over the clams at the next station, some older ladies glare my way and talk behind their hands. My sweater feels thicker than Mrs. Borse's fur coat. I force myself to wave.

They stop talking and hurry away, their plastic clam bags swinging at their sides. I'm relieved when we leave the market to go back to the Hatterasks' house.

"Oh no," Yasmine cries. She slaps her forehead. "We forgot to do our homework last night."

Gomez shrugs.

"Can we go ahead to school to get it done before the bell?" Yasmine asks Nector.

But Nector shakes his head no. "The oysters will rot."

Gomez points at me like I don't have a name. "Send her home with the oysters."

Nector sighs and asks me, "Do you mind running this home? I'm not supposed to let them out of my sight since they went in the woods without permission."

I didn't do my homework either, but I've missed so many assignments Mrs. Dialfield probably won't be too upset about one more. I agree, and Nector hands me the oysters and his house key.

As soon as I take his key, I'm hit with the strong fish market stench even though we're far enough away that I shouldn't be able to smell it anymore. The oysters in my hand reek like they're already rotten. I rub my nose and bat at the air, trying to get the smell to go away. But I only succeed in making myself hotter.

Gomez's dark eyes frown. "What's she doing? She's acting weird."

The sun is sweltering, and I lean over. Sweat pours off my forehead in rivers onto the sandy road.

"Are you okay?" Nector asks.

I shake my head. I shake it and shake it, until the rotten oyster smell is gone, the hot sun is gone, and everything else is gone, too.

No Devil Hiding Here

I WAKE UP IN MRS. DIALFIELD'S HOUSE. SHE pats my head with a cool cloth. It feels wonderful not to be so hot.

"Look, her eyes are opening," Nector says. He and his siblings stand over me, watching.

I sit up on the bed. "What happened?"

"You fainted," Yasmine says.

"And no wonder," Mrs. Dialfield says. "It's far too warm outside for a sweater. It's already eighty degrees, and the day's just getting started. Why are you dressed for winter?"

I think fast. "I'm staying at the Hatterasks'. It's all I had."

"Couldn't you borrow a T-shirt?"

I shake my head vehemently, and the Hatterasks' eyes go wide.

"You're sweating, and you need to cool off," Mrs. Dialfield insists. "Here, you can change into something of mine."

She can't see my bite. She's got *Beware* posters plastered all over her front door. What if she sends me to quarantine? "No. It's . . . um. It's because I held Nector's key," I explain. "It doesn't look like it, but I'm cold."

"Oh!" Mrs. Dialfield smiles like we're sharing a secret. "Another reading?"

I nod.

Someone bangs on the door. Mrs. Dialfield answers.

"Is Spirit here? I heard she fainted in the street."

It's Dr. Wade. I don't have time to figure out what to do.

He takes one glance at me and declares, "This is a disaster." His voice is high, his face is scrunched, his hands are covered in rubber gloves.

Mrs. Dialfield looks taken aback. "I'd hardly call an overheated child a disaster."

"I'm okay." I jump out of bed. "See?"

"You could infect the others." Dr. Wade grabs my arm and pulls me out of the house.

"Hey!" Mrs. Dialfield says in surprise.

I try to wiggle free, but the doctor has a firm grip on my sweater with those rubber gloves.

Mrs. Dialfield runs after us. "Where are you going? Don't hurt her." Our teacher's face looks worried.

"I'm just trying to get Spirit away from the other children," Dr. Wade says.

"Is the sickness really that contagious?" Mrs. Dialfield asks.

The Hatterask kids crowd behind her, too curious to back away.

"My phone is ringing off the hook. I've got people who *think* they're sick, people who want to tell me someone they *know* is sick, and people who're scared they're *going* to get sick. Everyone is counting on me to contain this thing."

"But *I'm* not sick. I promise I'm fine." And I am. Now that I'm not touching any keys or smelling rotten oysters, I feel good as new.

The doctor gives me a suspicious frown, as if he's expecting me to fall over faint again. He shoos away the Hatterasks. "You kids get away from Spirit. Go on now."

Yasmine and Gomez take off. Nector lags behind like he doesn't want to go.

"Honest, I'm okay." I do a few jumping jacks and a kick.

"Well . . ." The doctor hesitates. "You don't seem weak." He leans in for a closer look.

I don't want him to examine me too carefully or he'll find my baldie bite. "If you want, I can run to the beach and back to prove I feel great." I jog in place and ready myself for takeoff.

"What? No! Don't go anywhere." Dr. Wade's gray eyebrows shoot up in alarm. He turns to Mrs. Dialfield. "I think this child should come with me."

Dr. Wade takes one arm, and Mrs. Dialfield takes the other.

"Her father is ill, and now she is, too. If I don't take measures—"

I interrupt the doctor. "Where's my dad? I want to see him."

Mrs. Dialfield doesn't loosen her hold on my arm. "I think you might be overreacting. I don't see any sense making a fuss over a child improperly dressed on a hot day."

"I have to do what's necessary to prevent the spread of this disease." Dr. Wade gives Mrs. Dialfield a steady glare. "Not that you've been any help in that regard."

They lock eyes over my head, and no one says anything for a few seconds.

"Do you really think it's so highly contagious?" Mrs. Dialfield asks again.

Dr. Wade nods.

"There're just a few days left of school," Mrs. Dialfield says slowly. "Perhaps you were right, and it would be best to discontinue class until this sickness passes. I myself have a weakened immune system, and the last thing I need is to catch this . . . thing."

Dr. Wade looks relieved. "That would be a load off my mind. It really would."

"Where's my dad? Can I see him?"

Neither of them answers me.

"The kids will be disappointed," Mrs. Dialfield says. "I was going to make sorbet for the last day of school, and lessons will be missed, but you're right—it's not worth the risk. If you'll allow Spirit to go on home and cool off, I'll allow the school to close early for summer vacation."

Dr. Wade turns to me. "I'm looking after your father, but if you're not careful, I'll have to look after you, too. Those baldies should not be pets, young lady. They never came anywhere near our homes until you took one in." His eyes flash. "You are not to call them near to us. Do you understand?"

"No, I don't understand. What's wrong with my dad?"

"He's sick, and I can't have him making anyone else sick. You go straight to the Hatterasks' house and put some ice on your forehead, you hear?" Dr. Wade warns. "And if you don't cool off, if you have any symptoms, any sickness at all, you call me right away."

"Go on, Spirit," Mrs. Dialfield says. "Hurry now. Do as the doctor says."

There's something about her urgent look that makes me drop my questions and get out of there as fast as I can.

20

HELPING MRS. BORSE

I RACE INSIDE THE HATTERASKS' HOUSE. MRS. Hatterask meets me at the door. "What happened? The kids told me the doctor—"

"I got away. I think Mrs. Dialfield struck some kind of deal to close the school to get the doctor to free me."

Mrs. Hatterask locks the door and helps me take my sweater off. "You're the luckiest little girl." She sits me by the fan. "Mrs. Dialfield helped, did she?"

I nod.

"Didn't like that woman much when she first came here. Determined to die. Thought she knew everything. Finally, I convinced her to drink our tea. Looks like it's made her well and given her some good sense, too." She sits back with a satisfied smile.

"Dr. Wade could sure use some tea. He was really furious with me," I say. I think of the old ladies who glared at me in the fish market, and Eder, who wants to send me to an orphanage. "Maybe the whole town is mad at me."

"Maybe you're mad back," she says.

"Me mad?"

"Sometimes anger's tricky. It can hide."

"Hide where?"

"Oh, it can hide under the veil of sadness or confusion. It can hide behind our eyes or in our hearts."

A telephone rings.

"Excuse me," Mrs. Hatterask says.

While she's gone I think about anger and

whether mine is hiding. I decide maybe it is. I'm angry Dad is gone, and angry no one likes the baldies. Maybe I'm also angry at death.

Mrs. Hatterask returns with the phone. She hands it to me. "It's for you."

"Spirit?" Mrs. Borse's voice doesn't have its usual gumption. She sounds shaky and breathless. "Can you come over?"

"Are you okay?"

"Hurry, child. I might not be for long," Mrs. Borse says. "The bird could stop circling."

Even though I don't know what she's talking about, I jump up to leave.

"Where are you going?" Mrs. Hatterask asks.

"I have to help Mrs. Borse. She's all alone now that my dad's not here. Dad gets her groceries from the market, and I'm not sure she has anyone else to ask for help."

"You shouldn't go out there," Mrs. Hatterask says. "I'll go."

"Mrs. Borse is particular about who comes over. I better do it."

Mrs. Hatterask doesn't look convinced. "What if you faint or get sick again?"

"I feel fine. I was hot from wearing my sweater on an eighty-degree day in June." I hold up my bandaged arm.

Mrs. Hatterask nods, still a little uncertain. "The weather *is* merciless."

"Maybe I'll just tuck my arm inside my T-shirt." I make it look like I have only one arm.

She laughs. "You won't look less conspicuous like that."

I pull my arm back out of my shirt. "I'll run superfast so no one can see I have a bandage."

"If you get caught with that bite, there won't be much we can do to keep you here. No deal Mrs. Dialfield or anyone else can make will save you, not with everyone so riled up. People are going to do what they can to protect their own."

"But I have to go check on Mrs. Borse."

"If you want to risk it, I can respect that. But you come straight back."

I tear out the door, not even stopping to say hello to Nector and his siblings coming up the street.

"Where're you going? You feeling better?" Nector yells. "They canceled school!"

But I keep running. When I get to Mrs. Borse's, she opens the door right off.

"You let me in on the first knock because I've gotten good at slipping in fast?" I ask.

"I suppose," she says slowly.

"So these devil spirits you're afraid will get in . . . are fat?"

Her fur hat tilts to the side, a confused expression on her big round face. "What's that?"

"These devil spirits I assume you think might get inside the house, are they large?" I ask, louder this time and into her good ear. Maybe if I had a mental picture of these evil spirits, I could understand why everyone's so afraid. "Are they too big to fit through the slit of a door?"

"I'll be. Fat spirits. I never heard of such a thing," she says. "You should be careful, child. The devil is always on the lookout for sassy children to snatch."

"Lots of people seem to want to snatch me lately." I shake my head. "But I doubt they can catch me."

Mrs. Borse lets out a laugh as loud as a baldie howl. When she's finished, she says, "You want to know why I let you in right away?"

"Yes," I say.

"For one thing, you don't have that devil dog with you anymore."

I do have Sky with me. He's waiting on her porch. Mrs. Borse just can't see him. But she's right, it isn't the same, as much as I wish it were.

"For another, I trust you." She smiles.

"I used to think you were weird, too," I say, because that's essentially what she's saying, that she thought I was weird. Or scary. Or both. "I used to hide in the honeysuckle bushes to watch you grab your packages."

She laughs again. "I know you did, child. You

think I couldn't see you and that baldie? Honeysuckles don't have tails."

True enough.

She has a pair of binoculars around her neck.

"What're those for?" I ask.

She jumps. "Yes! You've distracted me from why I called. Come see." She leads me to her bedroom, to the same window the eagle flew through. I notice the window is fixed now, and so is the ceiling where the bullet hit. She must have let Mr. Hatterask inside. I wonder if he made himself flat and fast. Outside, the eagle circles the sky.

"Are you worried she's going to fly in?" I ask.

"No, child. She's learned her lesson on that. We have an understanding now. She's come to warn me."

"Warn you? Of what?"

"This." She hands me the binoculars. "Look there, next to that clump of trees."

I put the binoculars to my eyes, and there's a baldie lying on the ground not moving. A fifth. I lower the binoculars, my heart heavy. How many more will die? What if the whole island of baldies is wiped out?

"Will you burn it for me?" Mrs. Borse asks.

"We can do it together."

"If you won't be reasonable, I'll burn him from here." Mrs. Borse fetches a book of matches from the top drawer of her bureau and pinches off a stick. She strikes it and picks up a lace doily the lamp used to sit on. She holds the cloth above the flame, and I realize she plans to light it and take aim through the window.

I grab her arm. "Stop! You'll set the whole island on fire." I remember my vision and Dad's. Is this how the fires start?

She lowers her hand. "Better than letting the devil inside. I don't know how long the bird will circle. If she leaves, I'm doomed. There will be nothing between me and that devil spirit."

And *I'm* the one who's unreasonable? But of course I agree to burn the baldie for her.

"Thank you, child. It's only you who can help us. You have a way with those beasts. I wouldn't throw you to the baldies if I thought otherwise. I'm much too fond of you for that." She grabs me into a fierce hug.

Mrs. Borse is crazier than wasps in a sand-storm, but I hug her back.

SMELLING THE FUTURE

HOME IS ONLY A FEW STEPS AWAY, SO I STOP there to rummage through our supplies. I took Mrs. Borse's matches, but I didn't ask her for gloves or a pallet. I have to safely burn the baldie and prevent a fire-filled future.

But as soon as I walk through the door, I realize all Dad's boxes are missing. Even if I couldn't see it with my own eyes, I can smell that someone else has been here. Someone who smells a sticky kind of sweet.

I search the house, but every box is gone. We've been cleaned out. I stick my head in the freezer to get rid of the rotten, sweaty feeling that overwhelms me. Who would have stolen Dad's supplies?

We keep a spare key under a rock by the door. Everyone keeps keys hidden on their porch. Mrs. Hatterask obviously figured it out when she picked up my clothes for me. If you steal something from someone on this island, unless you bury it, everyone will know soon enough. And if you have Mrs. Borse as a neighbor, you can find out right away.

Mrs. Borse is the best security camera money can't buy. I run back to her house. "Mrs. Borse!" I scream through the door.

She doesn't hesitate to make a sliver for me to slip through. "Our stuff is gone," I say, breathless and scared.

She nods.

"Did you see? Who took it?"

The binoculars are still around her neck. "Eder. He came last night. Made ten trips with that truck of his, I'd say. You didn't know he was comin'?"

I shake my head. Eder already has the money to buy whatever he needs. Why would he take our stuff?

"Probably hauling it over for your dad at the whale station," Mrs. Borse muses. "Don't you think?"

"I don't know, but I'm going to find out."

"I'm sure you will. You're a resourceful child. But first you best rid me of that devil."

Mrs. Borse gathers the supplies I need, and I leave to burn the fifth dead baldie.

AT THE HATTERASKS', NECTOR IS TRYING TO mess up Yasmine and Gomez's paddle rhythm by throwing the toy airplane he got from the cereal box over the ball. But Yasmine and Gomez keep to the beat. Their concentration is intense— until Gomez sees me and misses. "Why do you have to sneak up on people like that?" he demands.

I shrug, because I didn't do it on purpose.

"A moving object didn't faze you, but Spirit just standing there made you miss?" Nector asks. He seems disappointed that he wasn't the one to throw them off.

"She's creepy," Gomez says.

"Gomez!" Yasmine yells.

"I'm sorry, but it's true." Gomez throws down the paddle and looks at Yasmine. "She walked straight into that baldie cave without blinking an eye. You didn't see it like I did."

"I had a reason," I say.

They stare at me waiting to hear it, but telling them I was following a ghost dog won't make me any less creepy. So I don't say why. Instead, I raise my gloved hands, which carry Mrs. Borse's pallet, matches, and a blanket. "I have to burn a baldie or Mrs. Borse is going to set the whole island on fire throwing flames from her window."

"Another baldie?" Nector asks.

I nod.

Nector eyes my supplies. "Do you want help?" He takes the heavy pallet from my hand.

"You can't. Remember what Mom said?" Yasmine's voice raises an anxious notch. "We have to be careful."

"You're already a goner. Mom says there's still hope for us," Gomez tells me.

I ignore him and look at Nector. "Do you have gloves?"

Nector nods.

"If he gets the devil's sickness, it'll be your fault," Gomez threatens.

I don't want to respond, because he's a scared ten-year-old. But I can't leave it. When it comes to the baldies, my big mouth can't stay shut. "I don't believe they have devil spirits. I'm not the one who wants to burn the baldie. It's all the same to me."

Gomez's eyes widen.

"Why don't you believe they have devil spirits?" Yasmine asks me.

I pause, because I can't tell her I see their spirits—even the ones who were burned instead of buried—and they seem normal to me. "I just don't," I say.

Nector nods. "Okay. So we believe different things."

"Yeah," I agree. "We definitely do."

"Then why are you going to burn it?" Nector presses.

"Because Mrs. Borse asked me to. She believes, and she's afraid. I'm helping her."

"I'll help, too." Nector sets down the pallet and runs inside.

Gomez frowns and Yasmine looks worried.

Nector comes back with a pair of gloves, and we leave to find the fifth baldie.

It lies in the trees behind the Fishbornes', but I don't have to navigate. Sky leads us right to it.

The baldie is crumpled and still, like the others. She's a female, and there isn't a mark on her. Sky paces around the body, sniffing. I wish he could tell me how she died. Baldies must die naturally all the time. But Mr. Fishborne was right—we never find the bodies all over town like this. It's like the dog knew she was going to die and wanted to get away from the others.

"What are you guys doing?" Tomasena asks. She and Kelvin walk over from their house. When Tomasena sees the baldie body, she screams.

"She's not going to hurt you," I tell her. "She's dead."

Tomasena continues screaming and runs back a few yards.

"Don't touch it. It's icky!" Kelvin yells when Nector and I move to put it on the blanket.

"We have to," I say. "We have to burn it."

"Throw a match on it and run," Kelvin suggests. He's only seven, so he probably doesn't realize the consequences of something like that. Unlike Mrs. Borse, who should know better.

"We have to take it to the beach," Nector says, "unless you want your house to burn down."

Kelvin looks terrified at the mention of what I predicted. He backs away with his hands up like we'll make it come true on purpose.

"We'll be careful," I say. "We're not going to be the ones who start that fire."

Kelvin nods, but it gets me thinking. Who will?

Sky follows us to the beach. He watches as we put his relative on the pallet, light the wood, and push her body out to sea. As we're walking back, I'm deep in thought about how I'm going to get to the whale station to see Dad. I have to avoid the woods. But I need something sturdier than a raft to go around the island from the beach. Sky's friends appear. They dance anxiously at my feet like they want me to hurry up and figure it out.

"You know anyone with a boat I could use?" I ask Nector.

"Eder's got a big pile of boats, but he doesn't like anyone else sailing them."

I nod.

"Seems like everyone I know is still saving their money for one since the last hurricane. Mr. Selnick used to have one. His got wrecked. The Fishbornes used to have an extra I'd borrow sometimes, but it's on the bottom of the ocean, too. They've got the oyster boat, but they use that every day for fishing." He pauses a moment, then he says, "Yup, everyone I know is saving up for a boat but me."

"What are you saving for?"

"You'll laugh," he says.

"I will not."

"It's okay if you do," Nector says. "Everyone laughs when I tell them that I'm putting pennies in a pig to buy an airplane."

"A real one?"

He nods. "And I know I need flying lessons. And I know it's expensive. And I know I'll never have the money."

"Never say never," I say.

"You really think I'll fly someday?" he asks.

"I think so, but my ability is still developing. I don't see things so much as smell them."

"Smell them?"

"I smell the future. And I can hear it, too," I add.

"Is it like that for your dad?"

"No, I don't think so. I'm pretty sure he can actually *see* the future."

"Why can't you?"

"I don't know. Maybe my ability still has some kinks that have to be ironed out." I almost say I can see other things, but then I'd have to explain about baldie ghosts, and the one bouncing at my leg like he's been trying to get my attention for a while.

As soon as I notice him, Sky looks up with his *Follow me* stare and darts off deep into the woods. His friends turn their eyes on me, too, willing me to follow. Of course I can't, so I clutch Sky's tag and silently call him to appear back at my side. But there're some kinks in my abilities all right. My favorite baldie's *on* switch is broken yet again.

THE CALL OF THE WOODS

I KEEP CALLING SKY WITH HIS TAG, BUT HE doesn't come back. I get mad enough to think harder about why he might disobey.

Back when I was little, the first time Sky laid eyes on the Selnicks' horse, he protected me so fiercely Dad had to pick him up and carry him away from it to get him to listen. The horse was big and unfamiliar, and Sky was convinced it was dangerous. What is he convinced is dangerous now?

I can't follow him into the woods to find out. I'm so worried when I go to sleep that night at the Hatterasks' house, I dream of the baldies. I think the heat is the sun beating on my shoulders, and all I want is to tuck inside their cave, where it's cool and refreshing. But the baldies bark, sharp and angry, louder and louder, until I wake with a start and realize they're not a dream. They're outside the window.

They surround the Hatterasks' house. Four ghost baldies, heads back, noses to the sky, throats constricting, howling. What do they want? Are they here to warn me? There are only four when there should be five, because Sky is missing. So I touch his tag and hope for the best. This time he comes, and I say an inner cheer.

Yasmine is sleeping soundly. She can't hear the barking. They're so loud, I wish I couldn't either.

"Can you make your friends be quiet?" I ask Sky.

But he joins his friends in the noise. It's hard to tell if he's helping me or them.

Sky barks on and on, but the baldies won't be hushed. I'm not sure what makes these wild baldies appear or disappear. When he chooses to obey, Sky is controlled by his tag, which is engraved with his name and my phone number. When I release it, he goes away. But his friends don't have tags.

My dream.

The woods. The baldies' home.

I also thought of the woods at school before I threw up and when I wondered how to get around the woods to Dad. Sky's tag is connected to his home. And the woods are the wild baldies' home. This must be how I made them appear.

But when I try to send them back home like I did with the eagle, they won't leave. *Go home,* I think. But they only howl louder. Since thinking of the woods makes them appear, maybe I have to *not* think of the woods to make them disappear. But *not* thinking of a thing once you've thought of it is like going to the beach and trying not to get sandy.

I get dressed and tiptoe outside the house. "Why'd you have to wait until the middle of the night to try to tell me something?" I ask them.

They get quiet. I've come outside, so they reward me with their silence. But it's only because they want me to follow them. They lead me across the island to the edge of the woods, where they wait. Their eyes are filled with that intense urgency that says *Follow me*. It's hard not to be taken in by it. There's something in the woods they want to show me, but I don't think it's as harmless as a horse. I think it's something actually dangerous.

Behind me, something smacks to the ground and a light goes bouncing. I spin around. It's Nector. He's followed me and dropped his flashlight. He raises a tentative hand. A guilty wave, like he's the one caught instead of me. "Hi," he whispers.

"You followed me?"

He nods. "Can I come? If you're going to the baldie cave, you shouldn't go alone," he warns.

"What makes you think I'm going to the baldie cave?"

"I thought it might keep calling."

I nod, surprised that his reasoning is pretty close to the truth. "How did you know . . . that it would keep calling?"

Nector shrugs. "It's how things work. If something's after you, it doesn't usually go away."

I consider this theory. The hurricanes hit the Hatterask house over and over, generation after generation. Nector's great-grandfather was called into the ocean during a storm. Maybe more than once until he couldn't resist it. Maybe I'm being called to the baldie cave. Maybe this is how legends are born.

I turn to Sky. *Is that where we're going? The baldie cave?*

Sky can't answer. He can only ask that I follow.

My wound isn't even healed. I can get hurt. I'm scared to go to the baldie cave. But if I don't find out what the ghost baldies want, I may never sleep again.

"You can come with me if you want," I tell Nector. "But it probably isn't safe."

"I assumed there'd be danger." He smiles a little and holds up something shaped like a wishbone. "I brought my slingshot."

"You can't bring it," I insist. "I know Yasmine helped me with that pellet gun, but . . ." I can't be responsible for hurting another baldie. I hated seeing the one that bit me limp back into his cave. It's not like the baldies can get medicine and a bandage, like I can. If they get hurt, they could die. "Leave it here, and I'll let you come."

"But—"

"No weapon. That's my rule." I fold my arms like I mean business. I hate to be bossy, but weapons hurt animals.

"Okay," Nector agrees. He runs the slingshot back to the house and leaves it there.

The baldies wag their tails, excited we've decided to play Follow the Baldie, now the most dangerous game on Bald Island. Nector shines his flashlight into the trees, and I lead by following the baldie pack.

I think of Nector's great-grandfather again. "If it gets too scary, we can turn back. I don't want to be led to my death."

"Me either. Especially since you wouldn't let me bring my slingshot." Nector gives me a side-long glance.

"Are you pouting, Nector Hatterask?" I demand, because if he's going to whine the whole way, he can go back.

"I just wanted to be able to protect you," he says.

I put my hands on my hips. "I don't need protection."

"Everyone needs a friend to watch their back," he says.

It's so nice it stuns me speechless.

The baldies pick up the pace. The trees thicken and the only light is from Nector's flashlight. It's so quiet that every stick that snaps under our feet sounds like gunfire. An owl hooting above seems an ominous warning. We don't get far before I don't feel so tough. I already want to chicken out and turn back. Suddenly the baldies stop, and I wonder if they can read my mind.

"What is it?" Nector whispers. We've stopped at a clump of trees.

"I don't know," I whisper back.

Nector swings the flashlight around, and I keep a keen eye on the baldies. The flashlight catches on something fleshy and red, and my heart sinks. I think it's another dead baldie. I take the flashlight from Nector and move in closer. But it isn't a baldie. It's a hunk of meat cut too cleanly to be wild. A steak from the general store? There's a strange liquid oozing out of it.

"What is that stuff?" I ask Nector. I wave him closer. The meat is covered in a bright yellow sauce. Its scent is sticky sweet. It's the same smell that was lingering in my house when I realized we'd been robbed.

Nector nudges it with the toe of his sneaker. "Looks like steak sauce from the future." He pauses, staring at it. "Or outer space."

I agree. The liquid is neon, not a color you

should eat. "What's a steak dinner doing in the middle of the woods?"

"Think someone was camping here?" he asks.

I swing the flashlight around, but I don't see any other signs of camping. "Doesn't look like it."

The ghost baldies have gone bananas barking. Sky puts his paw over the steak. He lifts his head and barks with a fury I've never before seen in him.

"It's dangerous," I say.

"How do you know?" Nector shines his flashlight, looking for what I see.

"Doesn't it look like poison to you?" And then as soon as I say it, I know it's true. This is what's been killing the baldies. Steak filled with sticky, sweet fluorescent poison that looks exactly like the stuff I saw leaking from Eder's car last Thursday morning. Eder is putting meat in the woods on purpose to kill the baldies.

The Key to Survival

I THINK BACK TO ALL THE TIMES SKY SEEMED like he was trying to tell me something—like the way he stood on his grave, strong and unmoving. *Is this what you were trying to say, boy? That you were murdered?*

Sky wags his tail and spins around like he's shouting *Yes, yes!*

"Look there!" Nector points to a flash between the trees.

I swing the flashlight where Nector points, and I light up a baldie. A live one. The animal crouches low like he wants to move in toward the free meal.

"No!" I yell at the baldie. "Get back." I wag the flashlight, moving my arm up and down, trying to create a barrier between him and the steak.

Sky and his ghost friends go crazy barking at the approaching baldie. They bang into him with their bodies, but their friend can't hear or feel their warning.

"Come on," Nector says. He tries to pull me away.

But I won't go, because the dog will eat the steak, making him dead baldie number six.

The baldie doesn't seem deterred by the fence I'm miming, waving the flashlight up and down. He moves slowly, gearing up to fight me for the food. I'm afraid to touch the meat with my bare hands. I have to guard the steak as if I've claimed it for myself.

Go home to your cave, I think. *Go home, go home, go home.* I close my eyes, chanting over and over, praying the *Go home* magic works.

Nector tries again to pull me away from the steak, but I stand my ground.

"Come on!" he shouts. "It's going to attack."

"I can't leave, or he'll die."

"Who cares?" Nector doesn't get it. The baldies are nothing to him.

"I do," I say. "I care." The weight of the truth hits me. I'm the only one who cares. And I won't stop caring. Not tonight. Not ever.

The baldie steps toward me another inch.

"Save yourself," I tell Nector. "I'm staying."

But Nector doesn't leave. His long brown hands curl into trembling fists. He bends his knees and hunches down next to me. He whispers, "Sure wish I had my slingshot."

I'm bent, too, over the steak. I close my eyes and mentally chant, *Go home, go home, go home.* I picture the cave, cool but cozy with a family of baldies. I can smell their warmth. I concentrate with a force that mentally transports me to the protected cave.

I don't know how much time passes, me frozen in thought, but when I open my eyes it's just Nector and me.

The baldie is gone.

I stare down at the fluorescent meat, wondering how to pick it up. We have to remove the threat. "We have to get this steak out of here. Without gloves, I don't think we should touch it—just in case the poison could hurt us, too."

Nector eyes the ground a moment. Then he takes off his shoe. He removes his sock and slides it over his hand, using it to pick up the steak. He dangles the meat from his socked hand, grinning. "Mission accomplished."

I laugh.

Nector slides his shoe back onto his bare foot, and we head back to his house, where we can close the meat up in the garbage can.

"I saw this same yellow stuff coming out of Eder's truck," I say. "I think he did this."

Nector nods like it's easy for him to believe. "If anyone thought they could control nature, it would be Eder. He told Mom once that she should do a better job fighting back against the hurricanes. Isn't that nuts?"

"Yeah." But even though I'm sure Eder put out the poisoned meat, I'm struggling to understand. He's our friend. How could he? "I found Sky's dog tag at your house," I confess. "It was Thursday, delivery day, when I came to your house about my broken bike. You know anything about that?"

Nector pauses like he's trying to remember. "Eder stopped by—I think it was the night before—to talk to my dad about building him a fence like you wouldn't believe. Said he wanted the tallest fence money could buy, like he was trying to keep out something. Dad told him that if he was worried about the baldies, they know how to dig under fences. Maybe Eder dropped the dog tag then?"

I turn my head so Nector can't see that I'm about to explode with angry tears. "Eder took all our supplies from our house. He took my dad. And he took my dog from me."

Nector nods again like he could believe Eder would do all that.

"But it's not just Eder who didn't like Sky," I say. "No one did. My dog was murdered. His soul was taken, but no one will care about making it right, because he's a baldie."

We walk in silence for a few minutes, unless the universe can hear my fury. "Should we tell someone about this? He has to be stopped."

Nector shifts his eyes to the evidence dangling from his socked hand. "Probably wouldn't do much good."

My fury grows because I know he's right. Since Eder is only killing baldies, people will probably say good riddance. "No one likes the baldies."

"I . . ." Nector hesitates. "I wanted to like your dog. I was working up the nerve to pet him. I was going to ask you if it was okay, but he disappeared before I got the nerve. You were always with him, so when you showed up without him I thought he was sick. I waited, but the next day he wasn't with you either. Then I saw your poster about him being lost, and I . . ."

"You wanted to pet Sky?"

He nods.

"No one ever asked to pet Sky." I pause, letting the image cool my anger. "He would have liked it. He liked you."

Nector blushes and shakes his head like he doesn't believe me.

"He did. I swear. Remember that time you were late to the docks because you were helping your dad finish painting at the Fishbornes'?"

"Yeah."

"Sky wouldn't stop looking toward your house, waiting for you to come. Then when you showed up, I had to grab his collar to keep him from mauling you with excitement."

Nector lets out a nervous laugh. "Mauling might have been a little more than I was ready for."

"I figured."

We walk more, then Nector says, "It was weird how that baldie backed off. It could have killed you if it wanted. Honestly, I thought it was going to." He pauses like he's thinking more about this.

"Sometimes baldies are hungry or protective, but that's different from being murderous."

Nector looks confused, as if he doesn't understand what I'm saying.

"People think the baldie who knocked over the tourist girl was trying to kill her, but he just wanted her sandwich. He was hungry. He wasn't a murderer. He didn't commit a crime."

"But if I killed someone for a steak or a sandwich, even if it was an accident, I'd go to jail."

"Baldies do what they have to do to survive. They can't go shopping at the general store for food. If they see a steak in the woods, they have to snatch it. It's like your mom. Despite what Eder says, she works hard to protect you from the hurricane. And if biting or growling at a hurricane worked to send it away, she'd do it. Don't you think?"

Nector laughs. "My mom would love that. She drinks two cups of yaupon tea every morning just to get through the weather report."

"But she's not mean. Not really. I used to think she was, but she's doing what she has to do."

"I don't know. I could see my mom getting excited about killing a hurricane with her bare teeth."

It's a funny thought, and I can't help laughing, too.

BUT THAT NIGHT, AFTER I'M TUCKED BACK IN bed inside the Hatterask house, I'm not laughing. Before Nector and I left the woods we found three more steaks. We used our socks to carry them to the trash, but how many more are out there? Eder's out there, too, a murderer on the loose, and poor Dad, an innocent man locked away from everyone he knows. And Mr. Selnick and Mrs. Fishborne locked up, too. It's not fair. Dad and the others can't be sick because of the baldies, because the baldies are being poisoned. How can islanders, kind enough to thank the soul of an oyster before eating it, sit back and let these terrible things happen? Well, I will not sit back.

I will stand up. I will find Dad. And together we will make things right.

THE GREAT ROPE

I DIAL THE PHONE FAST. "HI, MRS. BORSE, THIS is Spirit Holden. I need something from you. I'll be right over." I hang up before I even find out if she heard me.

But I guess she did, because she cracks her door and lets me in on the first knock.

Now I'm the one breathless and urgent. "I need a boat," I say. "Didn't Dad borrow one from you to clear debris from the ocean after the last hurricane?"

"That was a kayak. Beat-up old thing, hasn't seen the water since."

"You think it could make it around the island to Whales' Cove?" I ask. "I tried cutting through the woods on the closer side, where I could take a blow-up raft, but I got lost."

"Oh, child. You shouldn't be cutting through those woods. Isn't safe." She shakes her head.

"What about kayaking the long way around from the beach?"

"Be a heck of a lot safer than those woods. Got to be careful of the rocks with those strong currents, though."

"What rocks?"

"Big ones 'round that barrier island. Used to be talk of tearing down that old whale station, making a museum, but that was a fool's errand. Too many ships wrecked over there."

"I don't have any money to pay you back if I wreck your kayak. But maybe since you don't use it much, it would be okay?"

"Don't use it much? I never use it. It's probably

nearly wrecked as it is. Been lying in the backyard for years gathering dirt and bird droppings. A spin in the ocean might do it good." She leads me into the attached garage and points out the window to a sun-faded red plastic kayak leaning up against a fence.

"Your dad's the only one ever used it. Practically brand-new. I ordered it thinking I could convince myself to leave the house. I loved being on the ocean when I was younger."

"It looks like it fits two people. I could help you if you wanted to take it in the water. Not today because I'm in a rush, but another day."

"That's sweet of you, child. But I think my ocean days are over. Be careful in that thing, you hear?" Mrs. Borse says. "Wear one of the life jackets that're tucked inside. You don't want to meet your maker."

"I'll be careful," I promise. "But I can't control the weather or the waves."

Mrs. Borse nods. "Wouldn't expect you could, child."

I start to open the garage door, but Mrs. Borse's ear-piercing screech stops me dead. My finger freezes over the garage door button.

"Go out the front, please, and walk around," she says. "*Fat* spirits can most certainly get through a garage door."

I nod and slip through the front door.

But once I'm with the kayak, I realize carrying it to the ocean is a two-person job. The boat is too long and awkward, especially with my wounded arm.

I run to get Nector. If he didn't tattle about me slipping out in the middle of the night, I don't think he'll tell about me trying to save Dad.

But when I get back to the Hatterask house, Mr. and Mrs. Hatterask are sitting outside in the folding chairs.

"Look at this girl," Mr. Hatterask marvels. "First day of summer vacation, and she's up with the sun. Best time of day, isn't it?"

I nod, even though if I wasn't on urgent business, I'd still be in bed.

Mrs. Hatterask eyes my bitten arm. "I know it's early and most folks aren't up yet, but you really ought to be careful. Heard talk last night—folks wanting to build a giant wall to keep the baldies out. People crazy enough to try locking out the world, they're crazy enough to lock out a child, too."

"Now, don't frighten her," Mr. Hatterask scolds his wife. He smiles at me. "The other kids are still sleeping. Have you eaten?"

I shake my head.

"There's leftover oyster stew on the stove."

"For breakfast?" I ask.

"Nothing better than oyster stew to give you energy for an adventure." Mr. Hatterask winks.

His wife sips her yaupon tea from a mug. I can smell it from here. "Bet that bowl you had last night is what's got you looking so rosy-cheeked. I plan to have a bowl myself after I finish my tea."

"How do you know I'll have an adventure?" I ask Mr. Hatterask. I hope Mrs. Borse didn't decide to snitch.

"Adventure is what summer vacation is made for."

"Oh. Well, I'm sure I'll have one, then."

"That's the spirit. That's the Spirit, get it?" He laughs at his own joke.

A pang of sadness overcomes me. Dad should be the one using my name like that.

"Yes, indeed you are looking better," Mrs. Hatterask says. "But you best play it safe and have your summer adventure inside today. I'll run by the market when it opens and get some more oysters for tonight. Can't have too much when it comes to oyster stew."

The rotten oyster smell before I fainted! I realize the oysters she's going to buy will rot. But I don't know why, so I don't mention it. I hope the kinks in my ability work themselves out soon. Smelling the future isn't proving very helpful.

I may as well eat if I have to wait for Nector to wake up. No matter what Mrs. Hatterask says, I've got to get to Dad. I wish I didn't need anyone's help to move the kayak. But at least I have someone to ask. It's strange that it took Sky dying for me to make a few friends.

Two bowls later, Nector still hasn't woken up. It's not nice, but I bang around in the kitchen as noisily as I can. I wash the soup bowl and knock the spoon into it so it clatters.

But it's Gomez who appears, still in his pajamas, his hair sticking up on one side like a horn.

"What're you doing up?" he asks.

"I'm waiting for Nector."

"We don't have school today."

"I know."

"You wouldn't be up this early unless you thought we had school. *You* forgot."

"No I didn't."

"Did too." He laughs at me with his eyes.

"Did not." It's childish to argue, but I can't seem to help it.

He gives me a defiant stare. "Liar. Only a ding-batter would forget school's canceled."

My fury rolls in like a storm. "If I'm a

dingbatter, then so are you. I've lived on this island almost as long as you've been alive."

"Nuh-uh," he says.

"I've been living here six *whole* years."

"Six is a lot less than ten," he says.

"You were only four when I moved here. Just a baby. And I say I've been here long enough not to be an outsider anymore. This is my island, too. My home."

"You weren't born here. Your dad wasn't born here. And you can't change that no matter how long you live here. You'll always be a dingbatter."

I pick up the soup bowl and slam it into the sink so hard it shatters into a bunch of pieces. I raise my arm and crash the spoon in after it.

Gomez's eyes widen so far I realize I've frightened him.

Mrs. Hatterask comes inside. "What's going on here?"

"She did it." Gomez points at me.

I try to scoop up the broken pieces with a towel. "I'm sorry," I say. "I didn't mean to break it."

Mrs. Hatterask frowns. "You have to be careful. We don't have many bowls."

Her kettle of yaupon tea is on the stove. After I've finished scooping up the ceramic pieces, I pour myself a cup to calm the anger bubbling inside me. The tea shouldn't have any trouble finding it. "I promise to buy you another bowl as soon as I can charge for readings," I say. "I wish I could charge now, but I don't think it's fair to ask for money for smelling someone's future."

Gomez narrows his eyes at me as I sip the tea. "Why does she have to live with us? I don't like her," he says. "She scares me."

Mrs. Hatterask looks thoughtful, like maybe I frighten her, too. She puts her hands on Gomez's shoulders. "Spirit is our guest. And while she's here, we must treat her with kindness."

"It's okay," I say. "I was just leaving to start my adventure-filled day. *Outside.* I refuse to be locked up before I have to be. I'm sorry again about the bowl." I walk out of the house, but my fury follows.

Now I have to figure out how to move the kayak myself. I can't believe I was dumb enough to waste time thinking I could be friends with a Hatterask. My anger boils.

I should've had two cups of tea. Maybe the whole pot.

I touch Sky's tag, and he appears. "Please, Sky. Can *you* help me? We have to find Dad. We have to hurry."

Sky wags his tail as if he'd like that.

A great rope for a great moment.

Then I know: the rope!

I run to get it from my school backpack.

Once I have it, I make a loop in it and try putting it over Sky's head. But instead of catching on his neck, it falls right through him and onto the ground. *Come on, Holden Spirits. Why did you give me this rope if I can't use it?*

To unlock the magic of this great rope.

I think about the pheasant and the kibble, and how I had to put them on Sky's grave to make them part of the spirit world.

Sky and I run to his grave. When we get there, I drop the rope on the sand dune where Sky is buried. Then I try again, putting the rope over Sky's neck. This time it catches. I think of the woods, and Sky's friends appear. We run together back to the kayak.

I use the rope to loop all the baldies together. I'm so glad I decided to bury Sky. His grave is like a trapdoor connecting his world to mine.

I encourage the dogs to move forward by walking out in front. For once, I'm the one doing the asking. "Follow me!" I stare intently into Sky's eyes the way he looks into mine when he wants me to follow. It works. They pull the kayak like a sleigh.

We march through town to the beach in a line, and I don't think to wonder what our parade looks like to someone who can't see Sky and his buddies—until I'm spotted.

"Spirit, wait up!" Nector runs toward me, then stops abruptly. He stares at the kayak.

I hook my hand onto the rope so it looks like I'm the one doing the pulling. I'm not sure if he can see the rope or if it looks like the kayak is moving by itself.

"How're you doing that?"

If I tell him, Gomez will be right. I'll always be a dingbatter. So I don't answer.

I march on. I pretend Nector is the one who's invisible.

"Wait!" He catches up.

I can't run away dragging a kayak. So I stop. "Did anyone else see me?" I ask him. I shouldn't have gone through town like that, but hiding with a kayak isn't easy either.

"I'm not sure. Why? Are you on a secret mission?"

I nod.

"Can I come? I thought we could do something together."

"You want to do something with me?"

"Sure." He reaches his hand toward the kayak. But he pulls it back when he sees me watching.

I motion to the rope and the dogs. "What do you see?"

"That you're going kayaking?" He looks at me as if I'm Mrs. Dialfield, and he hopes he has the right answer.

I give him a stern glare.

"In a magic boat?" he adds. He grins like he wants the right answer to win him a ride.

"I'm going to find my dad."

"Okay, I'll come if you tell me how you're doing that with the kayak."

"I can't tell you," I say.

"You have to tell me or I won't come." He folds his arms over his chest. "That's my rule."

I frown. "I'm warning you . . . you won't like it."

"Tell me," he demands.

"What if I told you the ghosts of the dead baldies are helping me?"

"Really?" He looks stricken.

"Yes. Run away if you like."

"Why would I run away?" he asks.

"They're baldies," I say. "Spirits of baldies. Right here next to you."

"Are they nice?"

I nod.

"They're not devil spirits?"

I shake my head.

"Can I pet one?" He sounds amazed.

I laugh. "You can, but you won't feel anything."

"Where do I put my hand?"

I move his hand to the top of Sky's head. "This is Sky." Sky wags his tail. "He's happy you're here. He's wagging his tail. I told you he likes you."

Nector beams, and inside I'm smiling, too. I'm glad to have Nector join our pack.

AN ADVENTURE-FILLED DAY

WHEN WE GET TO THE OCEAN, NECTOR AND I stop to kick off our shoes. I untie the baldies. The wild ones jump into the water like they understand the purpose of the red banana-shaped object they've been dragging, but Sky runs off down the beach.

"Sky! Where are you going?" I chase after him, because I've realized when he does that he's trying to show me something.

He comes right back, carrying a folded piece of paper in his mouth. He drops it at my feet.

"What is it?" Nector asks.

"A note."

"What does it say?"

I read it.

> Most people are blind when it comes to
>   themselves,
> Face your today and you'll see for yourself,
> Your key holds tomorrow and a great
>   responsibility,
> Never forget the past, present, and infinity.
> We hope you enjoy this great gift,
> Granted you by the Greats.

"Your key holds tomorrow?" Nector gasps. "Is it talking about you?"

I nod. "My ancestors send me messages."

"Wowzers. That is so cool. Do they just drop out of the sky?"

"Literally." I pet Sky's head and tell him he's a good boy for finding it.

"Can I see it?"

I pass Nector the paper.

"What does it mean exactly?"

I read it again. "Maybe it's saying I'll be able to know my own future with my own key. My grandmother could."

"This is awesome!" Nector says. "Try it. Ask if we're going to make it to Whales' Cove alive."

I take out my key. "It's warm." I get excited, because my own key has never been warm before.

But Nector stops me. "If you see something bad, can we change what's going to happen?"

"As long as we have enough information to be prepared."

Nector nods. "Okay, do it!"

I clutch my key in the hand that's not holding Sky's tag. I ask it to show me what's going to happen. The metal is warm. The jagged edges feel sharp and strong, but I can't *see* anything. There's only darkness, and the smell of smoke.

I pause and try harder, but I don't get any visions. I seem to smell smoke a lot when I do readings. It's hard to *know* if it means anything.

The baldies splash around anxiously in the water. After a minute, they whine and cry, and Sky tugs on my shorts, trying to pull me in the water. "Stop that," I tell him. Of course, he doesn't listen.

"It's not working." I push my key back into my pocket. "I can't concentrate. The baldies are crying. They want us to hurry."

Nector looks at me intently. "Maybe you haven't faced your today."

"Maybe I haven't faced my ocean adventure!"

He laughs and wades into the water. "I'm ready."

I wade in, too, until the water is at my knees. I put on the life jacket and pass one to Nector. We pull the paddles out of the seat and climb inside the kayak.

I shove my backpack between my legs. There's barely any space, and I'm wondering how my team of ghost baldies is going to fit. But the dogs hop onto the front of the kayak, stacking into each other like Russian dolls. Despite their ability to pull the kayak with the rope, they're transparent and weightless. It's a relief. Otherwise we'd sink.

Whales' Cove is all the way around Bald Island near the woods. I dip my paddle into the water. Nector puts his in, too, and we're off.

It's hard work getting past the waves near the shore. My bandaged arm is still sore. I doubt I could have done this without Nector's help. Our clothes get soaked almost immediately from the water breaking over the shallow sides of the boat. I should have worn a swimsuit. Even a dingbatter should know you can't sit in the ocean and expect not to get wet. But I don't mind, because we're going toward Dad. Our arms circle around and around in synchronization, pulling the paddles until we're out of the rough tide and into the calm.

We pass where the old pier used to be. There're a few wooden posts—legs that once held up the pier—sticking out of the water without a purpose. Even though the pier has been gone a long time, the space still looks like a house without a door or a face without a nose.

Sky swivels his head, separating a little from the others. It's nice of him. He's checking on me. I relax and point the kayak toward the whale station.

As we get closer, we have to fight the waves again. The ocean shakes the boat, making it hard to direct. The baldies struggle to stay on board. A few fall into the water and have to scramble back up.

We're pushed toward one of the rocks that Mrs. Borse warned me about. Some of the rocks jut out of the water, but others hide underneath and surprise us. I use the paddle to push against them so the kayak doesn't slam to pieces. It takes every ounce of strength we have to shove away from the rocks.

Finally we get the kayak pointed safely and paddle to shore. We jump out of the boat before we hit the beach and push the kayak onto the sand.

"We made it." Nector grins. "Are the baldies still with us?"

I nod. The dogs shake themselves as if they think they're wet. I laugh, because they don't look wet.

We toss the life jackets into the boat and run toward the whale station. The rusty cauldrons that surround the ramshackle structure are as huge as the whales whose oil they contained. I'm grateful to have the baldies. They can warn us if someone is hiding behind one of the cauldrons.

We walk through an archway made of giant bones. "I think these are rib bones," Nector says. "My ancestors might have put these here."

I've never seen a whale in real life. It's hard to imagine a creature large enough to fit bones this massive. I can see why someone might want to make this place into a museum. The dilapidated building in the center of the cauldrons has a large hole in the roof, like a ghost whale seeking revenge took a bite out of it.

There's an open area that looks like a whale garage. It's big enough to fit one. There are gigantic bones in odd shapes everywhere, but no sign of humans.

"It's like a forgotten world of whale ghosts," Nector says. "Can you see any?"

I shake my head. "Look!" I notice the enclosed part of the whale station. "Maybe Dad's in there."

We run over to the little shack and call out.

"Dad? It's Spirit!"

"And Nector!"

Inside we hear Dad. "Spirit! I knew you'd find us."

But there's a padlock, and the door won't open. "Why is it locked from the outside?"

"Dr. Wade thinks we're sick!" Dad says. "He locked us in to save the island."

"But we're not sick!" comes Mrs. Fishborne's high-pitched voice. "Not anymore."

"Let us out!" Mr. Selnick bangs impatiently from the inside, but he only rattles the lock.

Nector and I yank at the door, but it doesn't budge. No matter how rotten the wood, the pad-lock seals the shack tight.

"We're trying!" I say. "We don't have the key!"

We circle the whale station, but there aren't any windows to break or other ways to get inside.

My brain is reeling. I'm not sure what I expected to find, but it wasn't this. I knew something was wrong—that Dad wouldn't willingly leave me. "We might have to sail for help!" I yell to Dad. Why didn't I bring a crowbar or something useful? Instead all I have is a backpack of school supplies. I have a lot to learn from Dad when it comes to being prepared.

"Maybe there's a key to that padlock stashed somewhere," Nector suggests.

I nod. "If you can't find a key, look for something to pry open the door. I'll check near the water."

But when I get to the ocean, I see something red bobbing in the water. Mrs. Borse's kayak. Oh no! We didn't pull it onto the beach far enough. We didn't anchor it. The tide pulled it out. I jump in, shoes and all, and swim toward it. But the kayak floats out too far, too fast. I'm a strong swimmer, but the life jackets are still in the boat.

The waves push me toward the rocks. One hit, and I could be injured or killed. I swim back to shore even though I know what it means. It's impossible to leave Whales' Cove without a boat or a raft. Strong swimmer or not, the close side of the woods, where I was going to cross with Yasmine and Gomez in the raft, is too far.

I hit shallow water and stand up. My arms are exhausted from paddling and swimming. The only thing left on the beach is the rope. Thank goodness it didn't sail away, too. I snatch it up.

I get back to the whale station and show the rope to Nector.

He smiles, and I'm glad the rope is visible so I don't have to explain. Nector holds up a curved whalebone he found.

I nod. "Together these might work."

We tie the rope to the padlock and then loop it around the baldies' chests. The ghost dogs line up, excited to play tug-of-war. Nector stands ready to shove the whalebone inside as soon as there's a large enough crack in the door. The baldies yank and pull with all their might. I yell encouragement. "Come on! You can do it!"

The door lifts away from its hinges, but not enough.

Nector groans and pushes the bone into the door, his face twisted and sweaty.

I tie what's left of the rope around my waist, adding myself to the front of the tug line. I dig my feet into the sand and lean.

Nector keeps trying. "I got the bone in!" he yells.

"I see it!" Dad calls.

We've made a small crack. Nector yanks the bone back, and the wood creaks open another inch.

I'm almost completely horizontal, inches from the ground, when the door gives way and my face smacks hard into the sand.

26

SHOWDOWN

"SPIRIT?" DAD PULLS ME UP.

I brush the sand from my mouth and throw my arms around Dad. Any pain I was feeling melts away.

I untie myself from the rope, and Mr. Selnick comes over. There's a healthy flush in his face. He looks so much better than he did when I last saw him. Dad does, too.

Inside the whale station, I see cots and

bedpans. "Were you cared for?" I wish we had something to offer, water or food, but when I look more closely, I see they have both.

"We're fine, honey." Dad holds me by the shoulders. "*I'm* not sick anymore, which means . . ." He looks at me, proud. "I think you've learned to use your gift?"

I nod and show him the great rope.

"How is it suspended like that?" Dad asks.

The others stare in wonder.

Mrs. Fishborne moves toward the rope, her hands outstretched, like she needs to feel what she's seeing to understand.

"These are good people," I tell the baldies. But I guess they know, because they seem okay with Mrs. Fishborne near.

"Who are you talking to?" Dad's eyes are filled with curiosity. Mrs. Fishborne's and Mr. Selnick's, too.

I'm wondering how to explain it to them when Mrs. Fishborne grabs my arm. "Look." She points at the ocean. A big boat heads toward us. The only person who owns a boat that big is Eder Mint.

"Maybe he'll take us home," Mrs. Fishborne says.

"I doubt it," I say.

Dad looks surprised.

"Eder put poisonous meat in the woods for the baldies to eat. Nector and I found some of the steaks. And part of my gift is that I can see the ghosts of the murdered baldies."

"Really?" Dad's voice is filled with awe.

I nod.

His eyes glisten. "I'm so sorry I didn't believe you. No one in our family has ever had a gift for animals. I should have realized this would be *your* gift. You have such a talent. The Greats wouldn't waste it. Is Sky here with us?"

I nod.

Dad claps his hands to his knees. "Sky? Come-here, buddy!" he calls to the wrong end of the rope.

I laugh.

"Sky? Here, boy!"

Sky leaps on Dad, licking his face.

"He's jumping on you, and you're getting kisses."

Dad smiles. "Am I touching him?"

I nod.

"This is amazing! I'm really sorry I didn't believe you." Dad hugs me.

"It's okay." I know Dad didn't believe me because he thought I was floundering—not dealing with Sky's death. He wasn't exactly wrong.

Mr. Selnick looks horrified. "You can see devil spirits?" His voice shakes.

"They aren't devil spirits," I say. "They're regular spirits."

"How do you know?" Mrs. Fishborne holds up her hands like she's trying to fend them off. "They could be here to harm us."

"They helped us break the lock, didn't they?" I ask.

Mr. Selnick and Mrs. Fishborne consider this.

"It's fortunate you can control them," Dad says. "Ghosts can be belligerent and uncooperative."

"The baldies are special," I say.

"Devils, all of them." Mr. Selnick shivers. "You can't convince me otherwise. You keep them away from me, honey, you hear?" Despite calling me honey, Mr. Selnick gives me a hard look.

Mr. Selnick and Mrs. Fishborne still aren't convinced the baldies are nice, despite being rescued by them. It's like Mrs. Hatterask being scared of Dad even though he rescued her kids. Why do people fear things they don't understand?

"I told you, they won't hurt you. They rescued you. You should be grateful," I say.

"We're not rescued yet." Mr. Selnick points to the ocean.

Bobbing in the waves behind Eder's ship is another boat.

"It's Dr. Wade," Mrs. Fishborne cowers. "We're doomed! He'll lock us back up."

We watch Eder and Dr. Wade anchor their boats. Eder gets to the beach first and heads in my direction. "Did you let these sick people loose?"

"Yes, because they aren't sick," I say.

Dr. Wade hits the sand and looks around in

confusion. "What's going on? What are you all doing out here?"

Eder nods in my direction. "I was boating around the island, bird-watching, and I saw these kids causing trouble."

My fury makes me bold. "Eder's the one causing trouble. You poisoned these baldies."

"What baldies?" Eder's head swings around looking for animals.

"Five baldies are dead. One of them is my dog, Sky, the best dog a girl could ask for. Did you kill my dog?"

"I killed the devil's creatures. Unnatural beasts," Eder says, and spits like he hopes he hits one.

There isn't enough yaupon tea in the world to cure my rage.

Dr. Wade's surprised eyes turn to Eder. "*You* killed them?"

"It's no worse than they deserve. Don't tell me you won't be the first to erect a statue in my honor when the island is free of them."

The baldies growl, low and deep from their bellies.

"You're surrounded," I tell Eder. "The baldies don't think you can be trusted. These dogs aren't the devil, but they won't allow anyone else to get hurt."

"I had to get rid of them. With your dad not seeing anymore, *you* couldn't be trusted to protect us from them."

I had no idea Eder was Dad's best client because he was afraid of the baldies. Eder counted on Dad. I counted on Sky. It's not an excuse, but it's hard when you count on something and then it's gone.

"It's only a matter of time before someone else gets hurt. The island will be a better place without them. They have to go."

The baldies don't like the sound of that. They move in toward Eder with the rope.

"Who's doing that?" Eder asks.

But the rope keeps coming for him. The baldies circle Eder, and I realize the potential. "Get the other side!" I motion to Nector.

I move into position and direct Sky to pull tight the loop in the rope.

"Sky, come," I command. He does.

Nector calls the baldie on the other side. "Come, baldie ghost buddy! Come toward me!"

The great rope tightens around Eder. Eder thrashes against it, but the rope is thick and secure with baldies pulling in either direction.

I untie a few of the baldies, then loop the extra rope around Eder's feet for good measure.

"Ought to tie up the doctor, too," Mr. Selnick says. "Lock the both of them up in the whale station and throw away the key."

"Please," Dr. Wade says. "I made a mistake. I misdiagnosed. What's a few days of caution to save the island? I was taking care of you. As soon as I was sure you weren't contagious, I planned to let you go. Let's all go home now, and we can sort this out."

"I'm not going anywhere with you," Mrs. Fishborne says. "And the only sorting out I'm planning is making sure you lose your license. Locking you up might not be a bad idea either. See how you like it."

"No one deserves to be locked up and left here," Dad insists. "Not for crime or sickness."

Eder and Dr. Wade are lucky Dad has such a kind heart. I don't know if I can be as forgiving.

Mr. Selnick wades into the ocean toward the doctor's boat. He raises an arm at Dad. "You were wrong about one thing, Holden. I'll never leave Bald Island. Not ever again. That must be what I said in your vision."

"Maybe," Dad says, but he's got a deep worry wrinkle between his eyes. "I think it's best Eder stay tied up until we get him back to the island. Then I'll call the mainland. Let them decide what to do with him."

I move to pet the space near Sky's head. But his fur flickers like a firefly. The other baldies flicker, too. Their murderer is captured. Sky and his friends will have to go soon.

I'll have to face my today.

I don't take my eyes off my good dog. I watch him as he swims into the waves, and together we climb into Eder's ship. Soon something I love will be gone again. Until then, I don't want to miss a second.

A Familiar Smell

WE'RE ALL ON BOARD EDER'S SHIP. IT'S SO packed with Dad's stolen supplies that we're a tight fit. Eder is tied on the deck. There's nowhere for him to run. But Sky and his buddies guard him close anyway, and Nector holds the whale-bone ready like a sword.

"Why'd you take our stuff?" I ask Eder.

"I figured your dad saw something he wasn't telling the rest of us. Wasn't sure what I might need for protection."

I look around at all the boxes. I'm not sure Dad knew either.

"I was going to give it all back. Replace what I used. As soon as the island was safe and free of baldies." Eder's eyes plead. "I was. Really."

"Maybe it's my fault," Dad says. "I wanted to be prepared for things I couldn't see, but I didn't mean to scare people."

Every time I look at the baldies, my vision seems like it's going wonky. They fade in and out. It makes me question if they're there at all. Without Sky I'm not sure how I'll survive. I could be like the pier, washed away never to be rebuilt.

It's hard to wrap my mind around the fact that I'm riding in a boat with the man who took my dog from me. The man who might make the ocean wave of remembering destroy me forever.

"Sky is watching you. He's going to make sure you don't kill any more baldies."

"Keep those devil spirits away from me." Eder shakes his head wildly as if he's trying to shoo flies.

"Stop that nonsense," Mrs. Fishborne cries. "It's ridiculous."

I nod. "Yes, fearing the baldies *is* ridiculous."

"She's right," Nector says. "Spirit can see the baldie spirits. They aren't devils. They helped us."

Mrs. Fishborne doesn't disagree. It's a small victory, and it comforts me.

I want to convince her and everyone else the baldies deserve to live on Bald Island same as anyone. They've lived here as long as folks can remember, but they're still outsiders. We have that in common. I don't care what Gomez says, Bald Island is my home—and Sky's and the rest of the baldies' home, too. No one has the right to take that away.

I watch Sky closely. These could be our last minutes. He faithfully guards Eder. Everyone here already knows I see the ghost of my dead dog. I might not have another chance, so I speak aloud to him.

"I love you, Sky. Nothing will be the same without you. Please don't go." I put my arms around the space where he wavers like a lit candle about to blow out.

Dad gets choked up watching me. His voice is wobbly and soft. "Maybe Mom can look after him now."

I nod, because I *know* she will.

Sky gets spotty. It reminds me of the spots I see behind my eyes after I've been staring too long at a fire. Then he starts to smell like smoke, as if he's going to disappear by bursting into flames. "Please, Sky. Stay. Just a little longer. Until we get home?"

His head tries to snuggle my shoulder.

I get the distinct feeling I've been in this moment before. It's so familiar I get goose bumps.

Sky's nose juts into the air, and mine does, too. He barks like he did in life at an unfamiliar smell. I look to the approaching island.

I've smelled this smoke. In my vision that wasn't so much a *seeing* as a *smelling*. If someone had turned on the light, I'd have seen what I see now: the island burning. Like we've been sailing toward a mirage that with a little sleight of hand has transformed into a giant swirl of gray clouds.

"My God," breathes Mrs. Fishborne.

It looks like it's coming from near our house.

"What have you done?" Mr. Selnick demands of Eder and Dr. Wade.

"Nothing. I've been sitting right here," Eder says.

Mr. Selnick shakes his thick finger at them but doesn't come up with any words. It's easy to see how he's speechless. We all are.

We sail toward a smoke-filled island. But no one asks to go back to Whales' Cove. We want to be home no matter the cost.

28

OUT THERE

THE SECOND WE HIT THE SAND, WE ALL scramble toward our houses. All of us except Eder. We leave Sky's murderer tied on board the ship.

Dad wants to follow Mr. Selnick to help with little Poppi. He predicted her life. She's his responsibility. "I want you kids to stay here on the beach where it's safe."

Nector and I nod.

But as soon as Dad's gone, I realize I have

someone to go after, too. "I have to get Mrs. Borse. She'd rather burn than leave her house."

I don't give Nector time to object. "Sky, take me to Mrs. Borse." Sky and his flickering team take the lead. I pull my T-shirt up over my nose and run into the gray swirl after my dogs.

As I get near Mrs. Borse's house, the smoke is so thick, I can barely see. Next door, the Fishbornes' house is completely ablaze. It looks like the Selnicks' house is, too.

Mr. Alberton, our volunteer firefighter, runs at me, screaming, "Get to the beach!" He dashes back down the street, and in the distance I see Mrs. Selnick trying to put out the fire with her garden hose.

My eyes water and burn, but I force them to stay trained on my dogs. The ghosts aren't affected by the smoke. It doesn't slow them down. I try not to let it slow me down either.

The trees in the Fishbornes' backyard crackle and break. The flames leap from the rooftop. The wind is strong. The fire will be onto Mrs. Borse's house any minute.

"Mrs. Borse!" I bang on the door. I can't stop coughing, and my throat feels like it's crawling with fire ants.

Mrs. Borse makes a sliver for me, and I slip in fast. I cough out the gray swirls for several minutes before I can get in a clear breath and speak again. "We have to hurry. You have to come with me."

She pats me on the back and pours me a glass of water. "You shouldn't have come, child."

"Do you have something we can tie to our faces?"

She shakes her head. "I can't go out there. No. Too hot today."

I ignore her insane understatement and grab two kitchen towels. I tie one to my face and instruct her to do the same.

She refuses. "You go on now. I'll be fine here."

"You won't. You'll die," I say.

"I'll be okay."

"There isn't time to argue. Don't you understand?"

She shakes her head again.

She's coming with me if I have to drag her by her fur earflap. Her house key is on a hook by the door, and I get an idea. She never uses that key for its intended purpose. It's hanging there for one reason. A reason I can use. "Can I give you a reading?"

She plucks the key from the hook and hands it to me. "When Mr. Hatterask came to fix my bedroom ceiling, he told me you're doing readings now."

I nod. Her key is warm, and for the first time holding a key, I *see*.

Great talents require great sacrifice

The ghost baldies are fading, but my visions are getting clearer. The key tells me I can't have them both. I won't be able to *see* Sky and the future, because Sky isn't a part of the future. But Mrs. Borse is.

"We should go upstairs," I say.

Mrs. Borse follows me to her bedroom. I *see* that I'll convince her there.

I lift the window and call the eagle to me. She's circling outside, and she comes along with the smoke. The gray swirls fill the bedroom.

Mrs. Borse coughs. "Put that window down!"

The eagle hovers. I point to it. "See that bird?"

"Of course." Mrs. Borse coughs again. "Now put the window down."

I close the window. "She was trying to tell you something, smashing in here like she did."

"What's that?" Mrs. Borse asks, her eyes curious.

With the key, I *see* and I *know*, and I'm sure of things I wasn't before. "She was telling you that the world is coming in here whether you like it or not. You can't shut it out."

Mrs. Borse looks through the window and tilts her head up at the bird. "What else does she say?"

"That she and a boy will help you get to the beach safely, and it's there you'll face your greatest fear." Mrs. Borse probably thinks I mean leaving her house, but I mean the baldies.

Mrs. Borse turns away from the bird. She gazes at me. "Will I conquer it?"

"Yes. But there's a price."

"What is the cost?" she asks.

"Your house." I place her key on the night-stand.

She sucks in a breath.

I remember what Dad said about giving people courage. I take her hand. "I promise, you'll be better off without this house. Your life is out there."

Mrs. Borse looks through the window again, as if to see what *out there* means. Everything ablaze, it doesn't look appealing, even to me. "You might lose your house too, child," she says.

I pull out my own key. I *see* that she's right. I place my key next to hers on the nightstand. "We won't need these anymore, but we'll be neighbors again soon. We'll get new houses and new keys."

Her eyes are intent. "You sure?"

"Yes," I say. "But we have to hurry. The present isn't something we can squander."

Mrs. Borse removes her fur hat. She places it in a hatbox in the closet. She removes her fur coat, and underneath she's wearing a red bathing suit—an old-fashioned one with a little skirt on the bottom. She hangs up her coat and takes a wide-brimmed straw hat from a shelf and places it on her head.

"Are you ready?" I ask.

Her eyes are nervous, but she nods. "I'm ready," she says.

I hand her the kitchen towel, and she holds it over her face. I offer my arm, and we run down the stairs. We run out the front door. We run until we're out. Out there.

29

THE BALDIES' FUTURE

THE SMOKE SWIRLS AROUND US LIKE A storm. Mrs. Borse clutches my arm. The gray clouds aren't as thick higher in the sky.

I look to the eagle and point. "Nector and the eagle are going to lead you. You'll be safe. I promise. Please tell my dad not to worry. I *saw* my future, too. I'll be with you all soon."

Just like in my vision, Nector runs toward us. "Spirit!"

"I need your help." I hand Mrs. Borse over to him. "Take her to the beach for me?"

He nods like I *knew* he would.

"Follow the eagle," I tell him. I run to the edge of the woods.

"Where are you going?" he calls.

Sky and the other ghost baldies flicker and cry anxiously at my side. They cry for their relatives trapped in their cave. I have to prevent the future I see when I think of the woods. A future where the baldies die because they're trapped in a home that isn't safe from smoke. The fire will catch the trees behind the Fishbornes' house. The baldies will retreat to their cave. They will inhale too much smoke. "I have to save the baldies!"

I instruct Sky and his friends, "Take me to the baldie cave." I dive into the trees, following the faint outline of their misty bodies. I don't know how I'll lead the baldies out of their cave, but I saw that I will. I saw myself on the beach with them and Mrs. Borse. It's up to me to lead them to safety.

The farther away from the Fishbornes' I get,

the easier I can breathe and the faster I can run. I crash through the trees. I don't care about the sticks that tear my skin.

My eyes strain to see the dogs. Only Sky's full outline remains. The others have faded to an ear or a foot, the glimmer of a jaw. But Sky is my good dog, and he performs me this last favor, leading me to the baldies' cave. He stands at its entrance, looking into my eyes. I stare back trying to communicate everything I feel: *Thank you, I love you, goodbye.* But when I blink, he's gone.

I don't pounce threateningly up to the baldies' home. I've learned from my mistake. I spot the orange backpack, which got caught in the bush outside the cave's entrance. Slow and quiet, I move to free it. The thick fabric has bite marks, but the baldies weren't able to get through the tough material. Thanks to Dad for providing the strongest survival bag known to man. I crouch down in the trees nearby, excited I have supplies to form my plan.

Great gifts require great talents

I clutch Sky's tag, but it doesn't bring him to my side. He and his friends are gone now. I understand they won't be back. All I have is a talent, the ability to speak to animals with kindness and understanding.

I open my backpack and remove an apple. I trained Sky with apples. I hope these baldies like them, too. I break a chunk of apple with my teeth and toss it. It lands about fifty feet from the cave's entrance. I follow the apple piece with a toss of the flashlight. It bounces heavily. I want to draw them out of their cave. They think it's safe inside their home like Mrs. Borse did. But they're wrong. I watch the cave, and I wait.

A baldie appears. He sniffs the air. He can probably smell me along with the apple. I hope I'm far enough away not to be considered a threat. The fire from the Selnicks' and the Fishbornes' makes a massive cloud over town. The dogs look to the smoke. I want to watch over them to make sure they aren't hurt.

I toss another apple chunk a few feet in front of the first one. The leader takes it. He looks my way. I toss another right to him so he'll understand the food comes from me. I keep tossing apple chunks for him and his friends. I back away slowly, luring the pack toward me. There are seven of them. I don't know if there are more in the woods or not. But maybe once we get to the beach, these baldies can call the others.

The pack of seven follows me. They could easily knock me down and take what I've got left: one more apple, a handful of carrots, and a small packet of peanut butter. But I move slowly, facing them.

I try to speak to them with my eyes like I did with the eagle and like Sky did with me. And I don't run like dinner would. I drop a bit of food, then back away. I do this over and over until the distance between me and the baldies becomes less each time. I've got a couple hundred yards to go when I'm down to the peanut butter. I scoop some onto my finger and hold out my hand. The leader sniffs the air, then moves in hungrily. He's not Sky. It took me a long time to teach Sky to accept food from my hand with a soft bite. I quickly push the peanut butter off my finger and onto the ground. The baldies dive in with gusto.

I lead them to the top of a sand dune overlooking the beach. Below are the people of Bald Island. I want the animals to stay on the hill, so I drop the backpack for them to sniff. They stop following me in favor of checking out the bag. They crowd around, pawing it and sticking their noses into pockets. I continue to back away, eventually turning to the ocean. I want to dip my face into the deep green-blue water.

"Spirit!" Mrs. Borse calls me over. In her bathing suit, she looks frail and small without her furs. Her eyes are wide on the baldies who've followed me here.

"Don't be afraid," I say. "They won't hurt you."

"I should've brought my gun." She looks around a moment, then clutches her heart in relief. "Oh, thank goodness someone has his wits about him and thought to bring a rifle."

Mr. Fishborne appears from the woods and

steps onto the beach. He raises his gun and steadies it on the baldies. A crowd gathers, pointing, and there are a few surprised screams.

I didn't see this in my vision. Have I made a mistake and led the baldies into danger? I jump in front of them. "No!"

Mr. Fishborne stands firm. "Get out of the way," he commands.

His wife approaches. She puts her hand on his arm. "It's okay. Spirit knows these animals."

Her husband turns. "What? Sweetheart, you're back! You look so well!"

"I am well! And I'm freed from Whales' Cove, thanks to the baldies."

"The baldies?" Mr. Fishborne lowers his gun a surprised inch.

"Spirit can talk to them and see their ghosts, and they helped me escape. I can't say I understand it all, but maybe we were wrong about these creatures."

Mr. Fishborne doesn't look like he believes it, but he allows his wife to take the gun from him.

I smile at Mrs. Fishborne.

Next to them, Poppi clings to Dad's leg. Mr. Selnick's face is black with ash, and he's wearing the blue plaid shirt he wore the day of Dad's reading. He puts his arm around his wife because she's crying.

But Mrs. Selnick isn't consoled. "There was a dead baldie by the shed," she wails. "I didn't want to get sick, so I didn't move it away from the house. The fire spread so fast. I thought I could control it. But the gasoline for the grill exploded, and . . ." Mrs. Selnick stops to weep. Her hand is bloody.

Mr. Selnick's face dawns with realization. "Honey, your hand!"

His wife nods. "I burned it. And I . . . I burned down our house." Mrs. Selnick buries her head into her husband's shoulder.

His blackened face is shocked. "We should've left the island."

"I'm sorry I couldn't tell you more details about your future." Dad shakes his head. "And I won't be able to tell you anything from now on." He gives me a soft smile. "If you need something, you'll have to ask my daughter."

People watch me curiously. Mrs. Borse doesn't look as wide-eyed as she did earlier. I wasn't able to save our homes, but I managed to save Mrs. Borse. And a few baldies. On the dune, my seven baldies have two friends with them. Nine of the island's baldies have made it to the beach.

"Are you sure those baldies won't get us?" Kelvin asks me. His arms are stuffed with superhero toys. He hugs them close to his chest like he's protecting them.

"You don't bother the baldies, they won't bother you," I say.

Kelvin nods, and the crowd seems to relax. People talk and hug. And after a few minutes, they seem to forget that there are nine baldies sharing the beach with them.

Nector touches my arm. "That reading you gave me," he looks into the sky. "I think it's about to come true."

Tiny black flakes fill the sky and our clothes. People brush at their hair and shoulders, but more flakes keep coming because a helicopter stirs the ash into a frenzy.

The helicopter lands on the beach, and two men who look like firefighters jump out. They motion for several people standing nearby to board. We're told there will be more helicopters coming. No planes. I couldn't see in my vision of Nector, so I didn't know the difference. I didn't know he'd be a passenger in a helicopter carried from a smoke-filled island. I turn to him. "I'm sorry, it isn't like I thought."

"It's okay." He smiles. "It already feels like flying."

I laugh because he's right. The wind from the helicopter whips my hair into my eyes and blows back Nector's clothes. His T-shirt and shorts look like they're caught in the whirl of a hurricane.

He lines up next to me and catches my hand. "Ride with me?"

His hand is small and warm in mine, and I nod. Our island is burning, but strangely, I feel more than ever like I belong to it.

We'll all be outsiders for a little while. Then we'll return to start again.

30

OUR FUTURE

A FEW WEEKS LATER THE ISLAND SMELLS OF lumber, and my ears ring with the terrible noise of those machines that make sawdust. There are more big trucks on the island than I thought I'd ever see.

The smells, the noise, the big trucks—they mean the people who need a house will have one again. Everyone is pitching in to rebuild what was lost. Our neighbors are in hard hats, and they raise wood into the sky. The skeletons of homes line the street. Nector has named the partially built wooden shells *spirit homes*. The insides of our houses-to-be.

"Got a new room put up in your spirit home," he says. "Want to see?"

I laugh because everyone can see. There are no walls. It's what's fun about today. Some tomorrow in the near future, things will go back to normal. We'll get new houses and new keys.

New keys. New futures.

Futures without fear.

Well, there's always something to fear, but the openness of how we live now and everything that's happened with the baldies has changed things some. People don't mention devil spirits as often, for one. While we wait for our homes to be finished, Dad's disaster supplies have come in handy. There's plenty of food and flashlights, and my job is to make sure people have what they need. We live in tents and shower in a facility we built by the beach. Mrs. Borse's tent is next to mine and Dad's. She's covered it in fur she had Dad help her order. Some things change slower than others.

Once a day Mrs. Borse comes out in her red bathing suit and straw hat to say hello and take her shower. I don't approve of the fur covering her tent, and when she appears I tell her so. We argue a bit, and then she hides away again. I asked her once if she minds us arguing, because I don't want to discourage her from coming outside. She said it's only real friends who disagree.

There are also mainlanders in green vests who care about the baldies as much as I do. They understand the dogs need protecting. I follow the mainlanders around and explain what I know. Together we create a fund called Protect the Baldies to educate people like Eder who don't understand the importance of preserving wildlife. We want to build a baldie statue in the center of town, too. We have a meeting about it where islanders vote *yea* or *nay*.

Mrs. Dialfield makes enough honeysuckle sorbet for the meeting to feed the whole island and probably half the mainland. When everyone's mouth is filled with ice-creamy sweetness, she reminds us that we all played a part in what happened. She warns that fear is contagious, and no one is immune, not even her. She says the statue will be a good reminder of our past mistakes so we don't repeat them. She also points out that along with everyone else, Dr. Wade and Eder Mint will see the baldie statue every day, maybe even from their living room windows. Mr. Selnick and Mrs. Fishborne cheer when Mrs. Dialfield says that, and they both vote *yea*. I can't blame them for still being sore at Eder and Dr. Wade. I'm still a little sore, too, but I drink my yaupon tea every day, and that helps.

It also helps that Eder donated money to replant the damaged trees, and Dr. Wade made a small donation to the Protect the Baldies fund. The mainland sheriff asked me what I thought about it, and I said it seemed like a step in the right direction to me.

Dad works construction with the Hatterasks like he did when we first moved here—before he earned people's trust enough to give readings. We've come to this moment again, only now I'm the one earning trust.

I can't give readings to those who want them

most, because those of us whose houses burned don't have keys yet. But I go around visiting people anyway. If they have a problem or a question, I try to help them. Mostly I listen, then I repeat the vision I had holding Mrs. Borse's key. I tell them how I *saw* our houses rebuilt. This is enough to make people happy. Dad says I'm doing a good job. I'm giving people the courage to face what lies ahead.

This is the Holden way.

The other day, Gomez handed me his father's key because, for once, their house was spared. He wanted a reading. I was proud to give it, because I'm not mad at him anymore.

I've decided being a dingbatter or not being a dingbatter doesn't have anything to do with how long I've lived here or how much tea I drink. I'm not sure exactly what it has to do with, but this is *our* island, and I have hope for our future. And that is all I *know*.

ACKNOWLEDGMENTS

THIS BOOK WAS INITIALLY INSPIRED BY Marisol, a dog who went missing. She belonged to my dear friend Anindita Sempre, whose faith that her dog would return to her knew no bounds. I have Anindita to thank for Spirit's faith in Sky and the baldies.

I have the magical Outer Banks of North Carolina to thank for inspiring Spirit's home of Bald Island. Bald Island is a fictional place, but I drew so much from the very real magic of the Banks.

Heartfelt thanks to the Ladybugs: Bridget Casey, Kristi Olson, and Hannah Hudson. You've been with me since the beginning, faithfully reading and critiquing nearly every piece of fiction I've ever written. I can't imagine my writing life without you. Even three thousand miles away, you give me wings, every day.

Thank you to Cecil Castellucci, who taught me that magic should have consequences and who, along with Sherri Smith, gave thoughtful notes on early pages.

I owe tremendous gratitude to Nova Ren Suma and her Media Bistro class. Nova asked all the right questions. I will be forever thankful to her for showing me how to outline. She helped me realize I could write some, outline some. For me, this back-and-forth was the key. I also owe a special shout-out to classmate Tara Oliveri, who asked all the right dog questions, forcing me to clarify what I wanted to say about communicating with animals.

Incredible thanks to the Highlights Foundation Workshop and my reader Rita Williams-Garcia. I pushed to finish this novel and make it worthy because I knew Rita Williams-Garcia (!) was going to read it. I will forever cherish the letter she wrote me, and especially thank her for pointing out that I could do more with Spirit's sense of smell. I'm also grateful to technical difficulties and the circumstances that led Rita to give Sara Crowe the first twenty pages of this book. I didn't think it was possible for two such amazing people to love my book in the same week, but the stars aligned. Sara is the best agent Spirit and I could ask for. She doesn't waste a second, and she found us the perfect editor.

Every writer dreams of having an editor like Susan Dobinick. Susan is that second pair of eyes with a sixth sense for what you're trying to do and where you're trying to go. She *knows* my book like Sky knows the woods, and her navigation has made the process more fun than work. She has a talent for asking that special question each round—the one that lets me dive into the magic of adding a new piece to the story, the one that gets me *excited* about doing another revision. It's been a heck of a lot of fun playing manuscript catch with her. And I couldn't ask for a better home for Spirit's story.

I'm extremely grateful for the support the book has found at FSG. Particular thanks to Joy Peskin, Kathryn Little, and Kristin Brophy for championing it and gratitude to Janet Renard and Karla Reganold for their marvelous copyediting talents. My adoration to Andrew Arnold and Eliza Wheeler for the mysterious and spooky cover, which couldn't more perfectly capture Spirit and Sky's adventures. Hugs to those who work so hard to get the word out about *Spirit's Key*: my publicist Brittany Pearlman and Lucy Del Priore and the rest of the school and library marketing team. And a giant kiss for Simon Boughton who made me a published author and was sweet enough to say he was the lucky one.

Enormous appreciation to critique partners Demetra Brodsky, Julia Collard, and Miguel Camnitzer. Spirit's story was shaped by your notes and enthusiasm. Extra thanks to Julia for her wondrous illustration talents. She created the lovely Bald Island map and *Spirit's Key* promo images that appear on my Web site. She also hosts spreadsheet-perfect writing retreats, gathering together Leigh Bardugo, Jennifer Bosworth, Sara Wilson Etienne, Abby McDonald, Gretchen McNeil, Nadine Nettmann, and Jennifer Gray Olson. Thank you to all the aforementioned ladies for friendship, laughs, and shenanigans. I'm glad to have you girls in my pack.

Love and thank-yous to my newest pack and critique group: Rita Crayon, Lori Snyder, and Frances Sackett. Our sisterhood has been such a *great* gift and your notes a *great* rope opening the door to a better book.

And thanks to Amanda Hollander, who was a reader and a fan when I needed it.

I would be lost without the Society of Children's Book Writers and Illustrators, an organization that has provided me invaluable educational conferences and friends.

Thank you to my mother for reading great children's books to me when I was little, and to all my family for their love and support over the years. Special thanks to my husband, Jer, who helped me imagine that being an author could be a real possibility. Without you, it might have stayed a dream. Instead, I'm living its sister, a miracle.